SILVERTON MYSTERIES
Jim Bornzin

SILVERTON MYSTERIES

iUniverse books may be ordered through booksellers or by contacting:

iUniverse
1663 Liberty Drive
Bloomington, IN 47403
www.iuniverse.com
844-349-9409

ISBN: 978-1-6632-5125-1 (sc)
ISBN: 978-1-6632-5126-8 (e)

Library of Congress Control Number: 2023903736

Print information available on the last page.

iUniverse rev. date: 03/24/2023

CONTENTS

La Peregrina

Invasive Species

Not in Silverton

Silly, Serious, & Sermonic

La Peregrina
THE PEARL

JIM BORNZIN

ADVENTURE FICTION – MYSTERY

La Peregrina is a famous pearl worn by European royalty and more recently by Elizabeth Taylor before her death. According to legend, the pearl has gone missing for long periods, only to reappear in another country or in a new royal family. The Spanish word *peregrina* means "wanderer, or pilgrim."

The author adds a new, fun, **fictional chapter** to La Peregrina's wanderings. The precious gem is found by a retired pastor who sets out to find the rightful owner and return the pearl. Unfortunately, before he can even begin his quest, the pearl is stolen by a pair of hired professional, but incompetent thieves, and the challenge of returning the wandering pearl to its rightful owner becomes humorously complicated.

Like the peregrine falcon, this story flies rapidly from one mystery to another, making it a book one can read in a day. Or re-read more slowly to savor and enjoy each twist and turn.

SILVERTON MYSTERIES features fictional tales from the life of Pastor Alan Johnson and his wife Traci. Expecting to live a "normal life" in the small, quiet town of Silverton, Oregon, they are little prepared for the unexpected and unbelievable, and sometimes unwanted events that ensue.

CHAPTER 1

LA PEREGRINA, A FAMOUS PEARL

E veryone in Oregon knows the name **Phil Knight**, founder and CEO of the Nike Corporation. Phil and Penny Knight have contributed millions of dollars to the University of Oregon, and to numerous other charities in Oregon. They were excited when their daughter Christina found the man she wanted to marry. Christina proved herself an excellent scholar at Stanford University, and then at Harvard, before becoming a professor of Art and Visual Studies at Haverford College in Pennsylvania. After breaking up with numerous suitors in California, it was in Haverford she finally met the man of her dreams.

One of Christina's close friends during her undergraduate time at Stanford was Jeanine Woodburn. Jeanine also came from a wealthy family. Her father, Mark Woodburn, was well-known in Los Angeles for the billions he had made in the movie industry. Jeanine's parents were not surprised when she came home from Stanford bragging about her friend, Christina Knight. During Christmas break she told them about being on the same intra-mural volleyball team as Christina. And during Spring Break, she couldn't stop talking about Christina's parents, Phil and Penny.

Finally, at the girls' graduation, the Knight's and the Woodburn's met for the first time. They were very comfortable with each other, and recognized immediately why their daughters had become close friends.

A few years later, Christina Knight asked Jeanine to be a bridesmaid in her wedding. Jeanine was directing a local theater production in Phoenix. The opening wasn't scheduled until October, so she agreed to fly to Portland for the wedding. Her parents, Mark and Janet, were also invited to the wedding. They were promised a most elegant welcome to Oregon. Mark and Janet were excited to see Phil and Penny again, and it would be a wonderful opportunity to spend some time with their own daughter whom they had not seen for nearly a year.

Mark and Janet packed their finest attire, including Janet's favorite necklace, La Peregrina. They were confident it would impress Phil and Penny Knight and the other guests. They would proudly watch their daughter walk up the aisle in front of Christina. When the date arrived, the Woodburn's flew in their private jet from Los Angeles to Portland for the big day.

The evening of the wedding, everything went as planned. Mark and Janet dressed at the hotel, and removed the necklace from the safe. Mark placed it lovingly around her neck and fastened the clasp. They reminisced again about their old friend, Richard Burton, and how he had purchased the pearl and necklace for Elizabeth Taylor. When it was placed on auction, following Elizabeth's death, they couldn't resist the temptation to buy the famous La Peregrina. It symbolized, not only their success in Hollywood, but also the many friends they had made there through the years. Those who knew them well would be happy they owned the pearl. Others need not know who the highest bidder had been. They would keep that anonymous.

The extravagant reception, hosted by Phil Knight and his wife, was held at The Evergreen on the southeast side of downtown Portland. Well-known for hosting such events, it provided a lovely atmosphere for dining and dancing. Mark and Janet Woodburn enjoyed the dinner. Toasts were made to the bride and groom. Shortly thereafter, a band was set up and began playing a variety of dance tunes, from swing to the big band era, from The Beatles to contemporary pop. It was nearly midnight when Janet suggested to Mark, she was getting sleepy, maybe they should leave.

They hugged their daughter, Jeanine, and wished her a safe flight back to Phoenix. Next, they wished Christina and her new husband a wonderful life together, and before leaving the hall, thanked Phil and Penny for a fabulous evening.

The parking lot was well-lit, but perhaps because of the drinks they had enjoyed, it took a few minutes to find the rental car they had driven from the hotel. As Mark unlocked the car and moved to open the door for Janet, a burly figure emerged from behind another car and darted toward them. Mark tried to shield Janet from the charging maniac, but was shoved against the side of the car. Janet screamed as the man grabbed her necklace and gave it a yank. The large pear-shaped pearl came off in his hand. He took off running. Mark took Janet's hand and asked, "Are you okay?"

"Yes, I'm alright. He didn't hurt me; he just grabbed my necklace." Janet looked down to see her necklace dangling about her neck minus the pearl. "The pearl!" she screamed. "La Peregrina!"

Mark pulled his cell phone from his jacket pocket and dialed 9-1-1. He reported the robbery and location, and within minutes they could hear sirens coming from several directions. As the first squad car pulled into the lot, Mark pointed in the direction the man had run. He hollered, "The guy was young, maybe thirty, had a beard, and was wearing a blue hoodie." The car sped off in the direction Mark had pointed.

Soon, other cars were chasing the first, all with sirens blaring. Another police car came into the parking lot as guests came out of The Evergreen to see what was going on. The last police car was marked "Support Team." Two young officers in uniform, a man and a woman, got out of the car. An older woman, not in uniform, emerged from the back seat. She and the young man approached Mark and Janet who were now surrounded by other guests. "Is anyone hurt?" the older officer inquired.

"We're okay," Mark replied. "But a large pearl was ripped off my wife's necklace."

The support officer was gentle but strong, as she questioned the Woodburn's about the incident. Then she firmly ordered the crowd to move back inside, many of whom decided to head for their cars. As people dispersed, the officer suggested that Janet and Mark might also go inside and sit down a few minutes. "Let's see if our other officers report any success in finding the perpetrator."

It did feel good to be seated. The woman officer was a good listener as Janet repeated how terrible she felt about the pearl. Janet showed her the necklace and where the pearl had been fastened. Then she told her the story about its history and how fortunate they felt to have purchased it from the Elizabeth Taylor jewelry collection.

When the suspect saw the police cars approaching, he dashed toward the Morrison bridge and dropped the pearl over the ledge to the river's edge below. He hoped he'd be back in a day or two to pick it up.

Nearly half an hour had passed when the young woman officer, who had remained in the parking lot, came running into the hall. "They've got him!" she informed them. "He was heading for the bridge. They caught him on Morrison just as he was running up the ramp. They've got him in the squad car now for questioning."

"Tell them to search for a large pearl that he yanked off this woman's necklace," the support officer replied.

The young woman responded, "They said they did a search and found nothing, but they are bringing him back here for a positive identification."

A few minutes later the police car pulled into the lot, lights flashing but siren mute. The support team escorted Mark and Janet back out to the parking lot. The suspect in handcuffs was pulled from the back of the squad car. "Is this the man who assaulted you?" one of the officers asked.

"That's the guy. I'm sure of it," Mark answered.

Janet stepped toward the suspect, "Where's my pearl, you creep?"

"Wouldn't you like to know," he taunted in reply.

"Frisk him again!" the senior officer ordered.

A younger policeman pushed the suspect against the car and began patting the guy down. "No sign of the pearl," he reported.

"Damn it!" Janet shouted as she began to cry. Mark put his arm around her shoulder. The officer ordered the suspect back into the patrol car.

The senior woman support officer stepped in front of Mark and Janet and placed a hand on each of their shoulders. "I'm sorry for your loss," she said. "If we find the pearl or any leads to its whereabouts, we will let you know."

*   *   *

Early the next morning, as the sun peaked through the tall buildings of downtown Portland, a large raven was walking along the shore of the Willamette River beneath the Morrison Street Bridge, when he spotted a large, shiny, pear-shaped egg. He picked it up in his beak and flew upward, landing on the bridge railing for a moment to adjust his hold on the pearl. Then he flew up again to the top of the Wells Fargo Center and dropped the pearl there.

After talking with his attorney, bail was arranged, and the street thug was free to leave the Portland city jail. He didn't mind going to court eventually. The brief assault on that wealthy woman was no big deal. His first job was to find the pearl he had yanked off her neck. He was mad the whole necklace didn't come loose. It looked like a beauty. But the pearl he was holding as he ran for the bridge was probably worth a small fortune, and certainly worth the trouble he was in.

Jim Bornzin

From the west side of downtown, he crossed the Morrison Bridge and climbed over the railing on the east side. The bank was steep and rocky and full of weeds until he reached the river. He moved slowly, looking thoroughly through the rocks and weeds for the pearl. At the bottom of the slope the water lapped over a mushy combination of sand and mud and scattered rocks. He scanned the mud for the pearl he had thrown off the ramp the night before. He walked from one side of the overhanging bridge to the other, but couldn't see the pearl. Several seagulls circled overhead beneath the bridge. "Goddammit!" he hollered at them. "What did you do with my pearl?"

Under the bridge's shadow he walked back and forth for hours, across the mud, and along the edge of the river, looking into the shallow water for any sign of a shiny rock. Nothing.

CHAPTER 2

THE JOURNEY TO SILVERTON

A ccording to **Wikipedia**: The brain of the common raven is among the largest of any bird species. Specifically, their hyperpallium is large for a bird. They display ability in problem-solving, as well as other cognitive processes such as imitation and insight. Common ravens usually travel in mated pairs although young birds may form flocks. Relationships between common ravens are often quarrelsome, yet they demonstrate considerable devotion to their families. Juveniles begin to court at a very early age, but may not bond for another two or three years. Aerial acrobatics, demonstrations of intelligence, and ability to provide food are key behaviors of courting. Once paired, they tend to nest together for life, usually in the same location.

Our raven, for the sake of this story we will call him Junior, had flown with a flock from Silverton north along the Cascade foothills to Estacada, then along the Clackamas River which joins the Willamette

River near Oregon City. The flock began to scatter as they flew north along the Willamette into Portland. It was mid-May when they reached the city. They had flown a distance of about sixty miles. It had taken them three or four days, with time out for feeding, resting, and just plain having fun.

Junior didn't care for the city environment, even though human food scraps were plentiful and easily found in trash cans and parking lots. Soaring beneath one of the Portland bridges he spotted a shiny rock on the river bank; his first thought was "egg." Not caring if it was from a pigeon or crow or even a sturgeon egg, he picked it up, but found it hard as a rock. Once he had carried it up to the top of the tall building, he set it down and did some pecking and clawing. It wouldn't break, but it was shiny and beautiful, even in his raven's eyes. *What a nice gift this would be for June,* he thought to himself.

June was the young female raven he had left behind in Silverton. He had been courting her for a couple of years, but they had not yet mated. His next thought was – *I'm still hungry.* So, he flew back down to the river to search for something more edible.

As luck would have it, he found a small dead salmon. The two seagulls at the site were no match for his angry caw. They circled overhead; otherwise, he ate undisturbed. That night he slept peacefully atop the Wells Fargo Center, nestled into a corner with the shiny pearl under his tailfeathers.

The next morning, he woke refreshed with only one thought in his small brain – June - not the month, but the female raven. He picked up the pearl and headed south along the Columbia River. Near the town of Canby, the river makes a sharp bend to the west. At that point, Junior veered to his left and headed almost due south. He stopped just south of Canby to grab a bite to eat.

Carrying the darn rock made flying more tiring than usual. That evening he encountered a good tail wind from the north and was able to glide into Scotts Mills. The area felt familiar so he decided to stop for the night. The loft in a barn on the edge of town provided safe shelter. He slept well with the pearl at his side. He woke when the sun came shining brightly into the loft. Junior stretched his wings, picked up the pearl in his beak, and took off heading south once again. Within the hour he spotted the old water tower on the south side of Silverton. Now, if he could just find June, he would present her with the pearl. She would certainly be as impressed as Elizabeth Taylor, when Richard Burton presented La Peregrina to her.

Junior tipped his wings and circled over Coolidge-McClaine Park. The human children on the playground swings and slides were shouting with joy. It was still early in the day. He realized June may still be up the valley near Silver Falls State Park, so he made one more pass over the small city park. As he flapped his wings to head east, the pearl fell from his beak onto someone's lawn below. He didn't panic. He was relieved to be rid of the extra weight, and now his mind was only on one thing - seeing June. He hoped she would not be soaring with some other raven. He flapped his wings more urgently as he flew up Silver Creek toward the state park. He just wanted to circle this valley with June at his wingtip.

CHAPTER 3

RAVEN DROPPINGS

lan was mowing his lawn as he often does on Monday, dumping the clippings into his green yard debris bin which would be picked up on Tuesday. School would be starting in a few more weeks, so he wasn't surprised to hear laughing and screams of delight coming from the children who were playing in the city park next to Silver Creek, about two blocks below their house. In the evenings, Alan and his wife Traci enjoyed sitting on their deck listening to the music of local bands drifting up from the stage in the park. Being a retired Lutheran pastor, he was free to set up his own schedule of maintenance jobs he did around their home. He often did "supply preaching" on Sundays, for pastors who were on vacation. And for the past six years, he had been mowing the lawn on Mondays.

Alan and Traci Johnson loved the little town of Silverton, just 50 miles south of Portland, Oregon. They retired there after visiting Mt. Angel Abbey, a Roman Catholic seminary, where they prayed God would lead them to a place to build their dream retirement home. From Mt. Angel Abbey they looked across the valley to Silverton, nestled in the foothills of the Cascade mountains. "Let's talk to a realtor in Silverton," Alan suggested. Within a week God answered their prayer. A realtor showed them a half-acre lot above the city park, with a view overlooking downtown Silverton. In the distance they could see Mt. Angel Abbey, and beyond that, Mt. St. Helens in Washington.

Alan had studied engineering and architecture during his college years, and when he retired, he pulled out his old T-square, triangles, and ruler, to design a hexagon-shaped house. Because of the large cathedral windows, he and his wife wanted a lot with a view, and now their dream had come true. It took nearly a year for a local contractor to finish construction, and another year to get the lawn established. Now, with the Oregon rainfall in the Willamette Valley, the lawn was flourishing and needed a weekly trim.

Dumping the last bag of grass clippings into the bin, a shadow flashed across the driveway, and Alan looked up to see a raven soaring up the valley of Silver Creek, toward the mountains. They were used to seeing crows heading to the farms to find food, then back up the valley to roost. The bird Alan watched was much larger than a crow, and soaring along on the updraft wind.

A white stone fell and bounced on the newly mown lawn, apparently dropped by the raven. Alan walked over to pick it up and thought at first it was an egg. Ravens will eat almost anything, dog food, peanuts, fruits and vegetables, even eggs. Looking down at the stone he was a little surprised to see how shiny it was, pear-shaped, and quite large. He bent down and picked it up off the grass. It had a beautiful luminescence, almost like a pearl. He rinsed it off at the kitchen sink and dried it with a towel, then set it carefully on the ledge above the sink. *Probably a stone from the creek,* he thought. *But I've never seen a natural rock shaped quite like this.*

As he was washing the stone, he was thinking about the raven. It had apparently been attracted by the shiny stone (wherever it was lying at the time), and upon closer inspection thought it was an egg, so he picked it up in his beak and flew off. At some point the raven realized he couldn't break it, and it was too large to swallow whole, so he dropped it. How crazy! In my yard!

Traci came back from the gym an hour later and saw the stone on the kitchen ledge. She picked it up and turned it in her fingers. "Alan," she hollered, "this is beautiful! Where did this come from?"

Alan rose from the sofa, put down his Sudoku puzzle, and came into the kitchen. "Well, I was mowing the lawn and this raven flew over and dropped the rock on the grass."

"You've got to be kidding," she replied.

"No, I'm serious. I saw the raven gliding overhead, and then saw the rock hit the lawn."

"It is really beautiful!" she gushed. "Do you know what kind of stone it is?"

"No, I haven't got the slightest idea," Alan admitted with a shrug of his shoulders.

"We should take it to a jeweler and find out," Traci suggested with a sense of urgency.

"Yeah, that's a good idea," Alan agreed. "I'll do it next week when I go to get groceries in Salem." He didn't feel the same sense of urgency, but Traci trusted he would follow through, eventually. She placed the stone back on the ledge and went to take a shower.

A few days later Alan noticed the stone above the kitchen sink and decided he should do something about it. A walk downtown would be good. You can walk anywhere in Silverton in ten minutes, more or less. He left a note on the table for Traci, picked up the stone and headed down the hill. The sun was warm; traffic was light. At the door of the jewelry store the sign posted the hours it was open: Mon – Fri. 10 am – 4 pm. Alan glanced at his watch. It said 11:17. He tried the door but it was locked. He peered inside and everything was dark. Oh well, the walk was good exercise.

The following Monday, Traci reminded him to stop at the jewelry store in Salem. The store was open when he arrived. A small bell rang as he opened the door. They had used this jeweler before to clean some of Traci's necklaces. The young woman at the counter asked, "What can we do for you today?"

"I have this precious gemstone, and I would like to get it appraised," Alan replied, hoping it was indeed precious. He pulled the gem from his pocket and placed it on the counter.

"O my gosh, is that a real pearl?" the young lady asked.

"Well, of course!" he said, somewhat shocked by the question, but not wanting to appear ignorant. It had the color of a pearl, but Alan thought it was much too big to be a real pearl.

"Let me show it to our senior jeweler; I'm sure he'll be able to help you. Let me advise you, however, that a complete appraisal may take a day or two." The woman smiled, picked up the pearl, and went to the back room.

A minute later the jeweler came out with the pearl on a small, soft cloth. "Good morning, sir. My name is Scott. This is a very interesting gem you have here." He paused a moment, then inquired, "May I ask where you purchased this?"

Alan felt a lump of panic rise in his throat. This was not a question he had anticipated. "Well, umm, I'd rather not say. Let's just say it has been in my wife's family for many years, and she wanted to have it appraised."

The jeweler nodded pensively. "First of all, this is without a doubt, the largest pearl I have ever seen." He turned the gem carefully in his fingers. "There are a couple of small holes on the smaller end of the stone, indicating it was once mounted in a necklace."

"Yes, I think I saw the necklace, many years ago, when her grandmother wore it around her neck." Alan was winging the conversation and feeling very uncomfortable. "I'm not sure what happened to the necklace."

"I'd be happy to do a complete appraisal if you'd like," the jeweler smiled amicably. "It'll take me a day to inspect it more thoroughly and do a little research. There are several famous pearls which have this distinctive pear shape. Please fill out this form to indicate you are the owner, the day you brought it in, and your request for an appraisal."

Alan felt a little uncomfortable leaving the pearl, but he also believed Scott was a reputable jeweler. He filled in the form, including his address, phone number, and email, and signed his name.

The jeweler placed the pearl in a small velvet pouch and shook Alan's hand. "Any time after noon tomorrow should be fine," he said. Alan smiled, picked up one of Scott's business cards, and left the store. He was feeling a little uncertain about this whole thing. He drove to the other end of Salem to get the groceries for the week.

CHAPTER 4

LA PEREGRINA IS FOUND

B y the time he got home from shopping Alan was a nervous wreck. He hoped to be coming home with the pearl in his pocket, and an evaluation from the jeweler for. . . maybe a thousand dollars? What should he tell Traci? Would she be upset that he left the pearl at the jewelry store? He came into the house and hollered, "I'm home!" Traci came from the bedroom and offered to help unbag the groceries. As they emptied the bags, Traci asked, "How did it go at the jeweler's?"

"Well, he was really impressed. First, he wanted to know where we bought it. Then he said it was the largest pearl he had ever seen."

"Wow! I thought it might be a pearl. So how much is it worth?"

"We won't know until tomorrow. He said he would look at it more carefully and have an appraisal ready tomorrow afternoon."

"So, you are going back tomorrow, aren't you?" Traci asked.

"Of course. I'm as curious as you are," Alan replied as he folded the last of the empty paper bags and put them on the shelf in the garage. He was glad she hadn't asked any more about the where-did-you-get-it question.

The next day Alan made a special trip to Salem, hoping and praying this next visit with the jeweler would go well. The bell above the door rang as he entered the shop. The gentleman he had met yesterday saw him come in and met him at the counter. "Would you please step back here to my little office?" Scott asked him. A few moments later Alan was seated across the desk staring at the pearl on the small, soft cloth. "Once again, my name is Scott," the jeweler said as he extended his hand across the desk.

"Nice to meet you again, Scott. My name is Alan and I live in Silverton," Alan replied as they shook hands.

"Now, about this piece you brought in yesterday. I'm quite sure I have identified this pearl, and you'll be amazed at what I learned." Alan waited for him to continue. "I'm still curious, however, about how this precious stone came to be in your possession."

Oh no, not that question again! Alan hesitated before answering. "Well, I wasn't quite telling you the truth yesterday when I said it has been in my wife's family. The truth is I just found it a few days ago, maybe a week ago." He really didn't want to say any more.

"You found it. You just found it. Lying on the ground or in the street." Scott was squinting in disbelief.

"Actually, it was lying on my lawn," Alan replied with all seriousness.

Scott burst out laughing! "On your lawn! On your lawn! That's a good one!"

"No, no, that's the truth," Alan insisted. "I really don't know why I have to tell you where I found it. What difference does it make?"

"Okay, okay. Here's the deal. This pearl is called La Peregrina, the wanderer. It has a long history of being lost and found as it 'wanders' from place to place and country to country." Scott took a deep breath and continued. "Have you heard of the peregrine falcon?"

"Yeah, I've heard of them," Alan answered, still puzzled. "I know they are small falcons that can fly extremely fast. That's about all I know."

"Yes, and they are found in most parts of the world. Maybe that's why they got the name 'Peregrine,' because they fly great distances and wander the world over. Anyway, La Peregrina is a famous pearl once worn by Queen Mary I. At least that's the story I read. Then it passed from one royal family to another, and was finally put up for auction at Sotheby's in London. And guess what? It was purchased by Richard Burton as a gift to Elizabeth Taylor for $37,000."

"$37,000! Oh my gosh! Is that what it's worth?" Alan asked with astonishment.

Scott laughed. "There's more to the story. Elizabeth Taylor commissioned Cartier to re-design the necklace, setting La Peregrina with pearls, diamonds, and rubies. And then in 2011, after Taylor died, it was placed on auction at Christie's in New York. It was sold as part of Elizabeth Taylor's jewelry collection, still mounted on the diamond Cartier necklace. Its value had been estimated at $3 million, but the bidding exceeded the estimate and reached around $11 million with fees."

Alan sat staring at the pearl. Eleven million dollars!

"And now you're telling me you found it on your lawn," Scott smiled and shook his head. After a full minute of silence, he spoke again. "The pearl was reported missing about two months ago. So, what did you do with the Cartier necklace?"

Alan continued staring at the pearl. This was not what he had expected. What could he say? What should he say? Was Scott accusing him of stealing the pearl, or the necklace?

Scott spoke again, irritated, "Where's the necklace?"

"What necklace?" Alan replied.

"The Cartier necklace. The diamonds and rubies. Remember? Your wife's grandmother was wearing it. At least that's what you told me yesterday." Scott's anger was building.

"No, I've never seen it in a necklace. I found it on my lawn. Just the pearl. That's all."

Scott couldn't believe Alan was going back to the story about finding it on his lawn. "I'm afraid I'm going to have to report this to the police. Will you tell me the truth? How did you come into possession of this pearl?"

Alan couldn't believe how upset Scott was getting. "I'll say it one more time. I found it on my lawn." He rose from his chair, picked up the pearl and the appraisal from the desk, dropped La Peregrina into his pocket, and left the store. *What in the world is happening?* He got into his car and drove straight home. *Wait 'til Traci hears all this! She won't believe it. I don't believe it. Eleven million dollars! Dropped by a raven? Well, maybe not eleven million. I don't have the diamonds and rubies and the necklace. Maybe the raven will come by again with the necklace!"*

CHAPTER 5

WHAT NEXT?

T raci was in shock as well. They looked at the appraisal which identified the pearl as La Peregrina, worth somewhere between five and eight million dollars. Together they had faced many strange circumstances in their marriage. People don't realize what pastors deal with from time to time. Yet never before had they faced a situation involving an eight-million-dollar gemstone. What's the next step? they kept asking themselves. Alan went on line and Googled – What to do if you find lost property.

If you find an item of property, we recommend that you **take it to your nearest police station or lost property office**. They should be able to securely search to find the rightful owner and reunite them with their property or investigate further if the item is stolen/linked to a crime.

It seemed like a reasonable thing to do. Alan got up from the computer and went into the kitchen where Traci was putting dinner on the table. He would talk with her after dinner about taking the pearl to the police station right after breakfast the following morning.

The phone call came that evening during their discussion about their next step. Caller ID said: BRIGHT GEM. Normally he would not have answered, but having just found a bright gem, Alan picked up the phone. "Hello, this is Sylvia with Bright Gem Insurance Company. Please don't hang up. I'm not trying to sell you insurance. May I speak with Alan Johnson?"

"Yes, this is Alan Johnson."

"Our company just received a report about La Peregrina, a very precious pearl. The report states that La Peregrina is now in your possession. Is that correct?"

"Um, yeah. I'm the one who found it. How did you find out about me?"

"My name is Sylvia Coeman, and I represent our company which had insured the pearl. I also represent our client who wishes to remain anonymous. The news that the pearl had been found came through the International Jewelers Association. May I make an appointment to visit with you in person?"

"I . . I . . I guess so. I suppose that report came from our jeweler here in Salem. When do you want to visit?"

"I've got reservations to fly from New York to Portland tomorrow. Shall we meet about three, tomorrow afternoon?"

"Yeah, I think that would be alright. Let me ask my wife. Can you hold for just a moment?" Alan went to the living room. Traci turned down the TV. They discussed the time for a meeting with the insurance representative. Alan returned to the phone. "Traci says that time works for her. Will you be coming to our home?"

"Yes, unless you want to meet me at the airport?"

"Why don't you just come here?" Alan suggested.

"That will be fine. I'll see you about three, tomorrow. Thank you for your cooperation."

Alan put the phone down and decided his visit at the police station could wait until after they had met with Sylvia. He jotted her name on the calendar. Three o'clock Wednesday.

That evening, feeling things might be moving forward, Alan and Traci sat watching a game show on television. Tomorrow, the pearl would go to the insurance company and back to its rightful owner. They heard a knock on the front door. Alan got up to see who was there. It was very unusual to have someone come to the door unannounced, especially in the evening. He peered through the leaded glass and saw two men, neatly dressed in suits and ties. *Probably Mormons,* he thought to himself. He opened the door. One of the men put his hand on the door and pushed it farther open. The other man drew a gun. "Step back," he ordered.

Alan did as he was told. The two men entered the hallway and shut the door behind them. Traci heard the door shut, and hollered from the living room. "Who was it?" Alan's heart was pounding.

"We're here to pick up La Peregrina," one of them said to Alan in a muffled voice, and waving the gun.

Alan turned toward the living room. "Just a couple of men who came to pick up the pearl!" he hollered back to his wife. Then, to the men he said quietly, "The pearl is in the bedroom. Follow me, but please don't let my wife see your gun."

"No problem," the one with the gun answered, "as long as you cooperate." He tucked it inside his suitcoat without letting go. Then he gestured Alan to lead the way.

Traci turned the TV off, then twisted in her chair to watch the two men follow Alan into the bedroom. In her gut, she felt they were not police officers. She was nervous, but decided not to say anything, just watch and listen.

In a few moments, the men came out of the bedroom and proceeded down the hall and out the front door. In a panic she waited for Alan to appear, and in a moment he did, looking white as a ghost. "What happened?" she asked as she rose from her chair. Alan walked toward her, put his arms out, and wrapped her in a tight embrace. She thought he might cry. She waited.

"They stole the pearl," he whispered.

"WHAT??!" she screamed.

"They had a gun. They said they wanted La Peregrina."

"And you gave it to them?"

"Of course. What else could I do?" Alan asked, shaking his head in disbelief. "They had a gun."

"Yeah, you said that," Traci replied. "I guess you had to do what they said."

For a minute, neither could say anything. They just tried to calm down. "Now what?" Alan asked, still shaking.

"Call the police," Traci said calmly, but insistently.

"I guess that's all we can do," Alan said, as he moved in a daze toward the phone. "Darn, I should look outside to see what kind of car they're driving."

"I hope they don't turn around and shoot you," Traci warned.

"Yeah, they're probably down the street and gone by now." Alan picked up the phone and dialed 9-1-1.

Within minutes a patrol car pulled up in front of the house. Two officers came to the door, one quite young, the other perhaps in his fifties. A full report was filed, including a very vague description of the facial features of the intruders. Alan said he was too scared to remember anything in particular. Traci asked if the report should include the upcoming meeting with Sylvia from the insurance company. "When did you find out about that?" The older officer asked.

"She just called, earlier this evening," Alan replied.

"Are you sure that phone call was legitimate?" the younger officer asked. "Maybe she was calling to see if you had the pearl and set you up for the robbery."

"She sounded legitimate on the phone," Alan replied. "And she said she was from . . let me think . . . Bright Gem Insurance, which is what came through on Caller ID."

"Did you check to see if Bright Gem Insurance is a real company?" the older officer asked.

"No, I guess I didn't think of that." Alan was feeling incredibly stupid and vulnerable.

"We'll check it out when we get back to the station," the young man said, as he jotted the name of the company into his notes. "Thank you for calling right away. And if you think of anything else that might be helpful, give us a call. Sergeant Phillips and I will be in touch."

As the two officers were about to leave, Sergeant Phillips turned. "I just thought of something. It might be a good idea for one of us to be here tomorrow when this insurance investigator comes to your door."

Alan looked at Traci who was nodding approval, and then back at the sergeant, "Yes, that's a great idea. We would appreciate that very much. It would really put our minds at ease knowing an officer of the law would be by our side. And it would probably make for a very short visit, if this Sylvia isn't who she says she is."

"If she shows up at all," the sergeant replied.

CHAPTER 6

CHUCK 'N' DALE 'N' SYLVIA

The Benson hotel in Portland was easy to book from their office in New York. It looked like the kind of luxury they owed themselves. The 12-story hotel features walnut walls and pillars imported from Russia, Italian marble floors, and crystal chandeliers. Their suite on the 11th floor provided two queen beds, and the steak and lobster dinner had provided the energy they needed before driving their rental car to Silverton. Now, after the robbery, and safely back in their room, they could order some drinks and celebrate their success.

"Hey, partner, we did it!" Chuck fist-bumped Dale.

"I think it went pretty smooth," Dale replied.

"Once I pulled the gun out, that old retired guy did whatever we said." Chuck was proud of how easily they had retrieved the pearl from Alan and Traci's home.

"Now all we gotta do is get through security at the airport tomorrow and we'll be back in New York and get paid for the job." Dale was confident the entire operation would be a success.

"Hey, excuse me, but I gotta take a crap," Chuck said as he headed for the bathroom.

"I'll bet that pastor and his wife are taking a pretty good crap about now too!" Dale responded, eliciting a hearty laugh from Chuck, before the bathroom door shut behind him.

Dale picked up the phone on the dresser and called long distance to New York to report the pearl retrieved. After five rings, a sleepy voice on the other end responded, "Yeah, hello."

"Just reporting in, like you asked me to," Dale realized it was three hours later, almost midnight on the east coast. "We've got the pearl, no problem. Everything went as planned."

"Good. You'll be back tomorrow, right?"

"Yeah, we'll see you in the office tomorrow afternoon."

"Anything else to report?" The question was followed by a deep yawn which Dale could hear.

"Nope, that's it."

"Okay, g'night." Dale had been hoping for a more enthusiastic congratulations, but since he had wakened the boss with his phone call, he wasn't surprised the conversation had been so brief.

At the airport the next morning, Chuck declared his registered firearm as he checked the case in at the baggage counter. Federal regulations require firearms to be in a locked case. It was securely locked, along with the carefully wrapped pearl. No problem. The line through security and the boarding process went smoothly without incident. Ten minutes later they were flying over Mt. Hood and gaining altitude over eastern Oregon.

*   *   *

Briefcase in hand, Sylvia, from Bright Gem Insurance, moved slowly toward the check-in desk at LaGuardia. Somewhere over Iowa, her flight flew within fifty miles of Chuck and Dale heading back to New York.

Alan and Traci had a very restless sleep that night, in spite of the pills they took to help them sleep more soundly. Both were up at 3:30 a.m. Alan sat in the living room and did a Sudoku puzzle which helped make him drowsy. Traci had already returned to bed, but both found it difficult to fall back to sleep. The coffee tasted good that morning. They dressed and discussed what they might do to pass the time until the scheduled visit from Sylvia.

They finished a late lunch. and they were reading in the living room when the doorbell rang at 2:45. It was Sergeant Phillips, in uniform and smiling. "Good afternoon, Alan," he said as the door opened.

"Welcome, Sergeant, c'mon in. Traci and I are so glad you offered to be here; can I get you anything?"

"No thanks, I ate before leaving the station. A glass of water would be fine."

As they settled at the dining room table, the officer explained they had done some checking on Bright Gem Insurance. Their website appeared reliable, along with a Better Business approval.

"My partner Bill called Philadelphia this morning, and the representative said they have a trusted employee in New York, named Sylvia, who has worked for their firm for sixteen years."

Traci was listening from the kitchen where she was rinsing some dishes.

"Well, I guess that means she's legit," Alan smiled and shrugged. A few moments later, the doorbell rang again.

Traci wiped her hands on the towel. "I'll get it," she replied. Sylvia was dressed in a light gray business suit, a leather briefcase at her side. "You must be Sylvia. I'm Traci; please come in." Traci ushered her into the dining room and introduced Alan and Sergeant Phillips. The four of them exchanged a few pleasantries and got down to business.

"If you don't mind, the first thing I'd like to do," Sylvia began, "is inspect the pearl to be certain it is La Peregrina." She looked at Traci, then to Alan. There was a long, awkward pause. She looked finally at the police officer as if to say, "What's going on?" Officer Phillips looked at Alan, then at Traci, who waited for her husband to answer.

Alan took a deep breath, let out a sigh, and spoke. "You're not going to like hearing this, but I'm going to have to tell you. Last night, we were robbed. Two men came in with a gun and demanded we give them the pearl."

Sylvia looked back at Sergeant Phillips who was nodding affirmation. Now she understood why a police officer was involved today.

Alan started at the beginning, with how the raven had dropped the pearl onto the lawn. Then he related his experience at the jewelers and how he learned that the pearl was La Peregrina. "I went online to see what to do when valuable property is found in one's yard, so Traci and I decided we'd better report it to the police. But before we could even do that, these two guys in suits rang our doorbell, just after you called last night. They forced their way in with a gun and took the gem. We called the police right away. Sergeant Phillips here, and his partner, came last night and took the report on the robbery. The sergeant agreed to come back for our meeting with you this afternoon. I think that about sums it up."

Sylvia nodded and listened attentively while jotting the story onto a tablet. Finally, she turned to the police officer and asked, "So you never actually saw La Peregrina?"

"No. We didn't. We came after the thieves stole it and left."

"How do you know Alan's not making this whole thing up?"

"They were really shook-up last night. I can guarantee that," the officer answered.

"You can talk to the jeweler in Salem," Alan interrupted. "He saw the pearl."

"Yes, that's who filed the initial report about it, and how our company learned it was in your possession. What isn't confirmed is this robbery you're talking about."

"Oh, c'mon! We called the police because two armed men came into our home last night."

"Or . . . you decided that would be a convenient way to keep the pearl for yourself." Sylvia looked from Alan to Sergeant Phillips who had a questioning frown on his face.

"Why didn't you take the pearl to the police right away?" Sylvia stared again at Alan.

"I told you, we were so excited about finding it, we didn't Google what to do with it until we learned how valuable it was."

"Then why didn't you take it to the police office immediately?"

"We were going to. The next day, this morning, in fact. Then you called yesterday and said you were coming today, so we decided to keep the pearl in our bedroom until you got here, since you represented the rightful owner. How did we know those thieves would come last night? We thought no one knew about La Peregrina except the jeweler."

Sergeant Phillips joined the conversation. "That would mean the jeweler is the one who gave the information to the thieves."

"Unless," continued Sylvia, "the thieves also had access to the information which the jeweler sent to the International Jewelers Association."

"You're welcome to search our house," Alan interjected. "Traci and I have nothing to hide."

"Well, I appreciate your willingness to co-operate," Sergeant Phillips responded, "but I'd feel better if I get an official search warrant before I do that."

"Oh for heaven's sake," Sylvia sighed in exasperation, "they've already hidden the pearl somewhere else, maybe in a bank deposit box, who knows?"

All four sat in silence for a minute or two. Sylvia reached down to put her notes in her briefcase. "I'll be flying back to New York tomorrow to file my report."

"Let me assure you," Sergeant Phillips replied, "we will continue our investigation here. And if we find any new developments, we will let you know."

After a few pleasantries, Alan and Traci escorted both parties to the door, and breathed a sigh of relief. "Can this get any more complicated?" Alan asked as he shook his head.

*   *   *

Meanwhile in New York, Chuck and Dale were standing in front of the desk of Mr. Leonardo Dantoni, a well-known businessman. What most people didn't know was that he also led a crime syndicate. Chuck placed his locked gun case on the desk, pulled the key from his pocket, and proceeded to unlock it. This had all been so easy. He opened the lid to remove La Peregrina and his gun, only to find the case . . . empty. The three of them stared in disbelief.

"Okay," said Dantoni, "so where's the pearl?"

"And where's my gun?" asked Chuck.

*   *   *

Peregrine falcons can reach speeds of 200 mph when diving at prey. La Peregrina was flying at a speed of 520 mph on the flight from Portland to New York. At least that was the assumption of Chuck and Dale when they deplaned at La Guardia. Chuck's gun case came down the luggage ramp along with their two suitcases. They rode a bus to the parking garage and drove their car to Mr. Dantoni's office in Manhattan. How could the case be empty?

They made a phone call to the airline office and inquired if the gun had been turned in at Lost and Found. "No weapons of any kind have been turned in today," an official voice responded. Chuck hung up.

"Somebody opened the case and stole the gun and the pearl," Chuck declared to Dantoni.

"Well, shit!" Dantoni replied. "Get lost, or go find it. You're not getting paid a cent until I have the pearl."

As Chuck and Dale returned to their car, they discussed the only imaginable possibility. Someone had jimmied the lock, taken the gun and pearl, and relocked the case. It had to be an airline worker or airport employee. But at which end? In Portland? Or in New York? And why did they risk losing their job to unlock a gun case? Because of the black-market value of a ghost gun. Scrub the serial number off the gun and out to the street it goes. They got into the car to drive back to their apartment, talking the entire time about whether they could find the person who handled their baggage. Not knowing whether it had happened in Portland before taking off, or in New York when they landed, they decided it would be a futile search.

La Peregrina was on the move again, and who knows where she would turn up next?

CHAPTER 7

SCOTT, THE JEWELER

A lan returned to the jewelry store a few days later. He wasn't sure what he would learn, but being a pastor, he felt he had a good understanding of human character. He would question Scott about the pearl, and about how many people knew it was in Alan's possession. He wondered if Scott had sent the crooks who knew the pearl was in his house. But he didn't want to tell Scott about the robbery. He wanted to allow Scott to think he still had it.

The bell rang as he entered the store. The young lady met him at the counter. Alan asked if he could speak with Scott. She told him Scott was busy, but she would tell him Alan wanted to talk to him. A few moments later, Scott came to the counter, smiling. "Ah, my friend with the pearl."

"Yes, I'm sorry I left the store so abruptly last time," Alan did his best to be cordial and sincere. "I came back because I wanted to thank you for the appraisal you did on La Peregrina."

"It isn't every day I see such a famous gem," Scott replied. He debated whether or not to tell Alan he had not filed a police report. He had been too busy filing a report with the International Jewelers Association. And although the gem had been stolen, he didn't think Alan was the kind of guy who would steal it. He seemed too naïve.

"And I'm sorry I didn't explain my situation better," Alan answered. "Nothing like this has ever happened to me before. I'm sorry if I seemed evasive, and I know it's a crazy story. My wife and I have been talking about this and decided it would be best if I just turned the gem over to the police."

"Yeah, that's probably the best thing to do." Scott was staring intently. He was also sizing up this crack-pot who said he found the pearl on his lawn. "So, did you? Take it to the police?"

"Let me ask you, did you tell the police I had the pearl? Did you make a report?" Alan asked.

"Of course," Scott replied, lying boldly. "It was a stolen gem. What else could I do?"

"Did you tell anyone else I had the pearl?" Alan continued.

"Of course not. Why would I?"

It seemed to Alan that Scott was telling the truth. He was a jeweler and ought to be trusted. He had cleaned Traci's jewelry in the past without incident. He had been in business a long time. Maybe it was time to tell Scott the rest of the story. He began reluctantly, "I returned home after learning from you, that La Peregrina was a famous pearl worth a fortune. I told my wife about it, and she agreed we should simply turn it over to the police, especially since you told me it had been stolen. I was going to take it to the police the next day, but that evening, there was a knock on the door. Two men, armed with a gun, came into our home, and stole the jewel from our bedroom. I called the police immediately. They came and made out a full burglary report, and as far as I know, they are still looking for those two men."

Scott stood in silence, simply shaking his head in continued disbelief. *If this guy really is a retired pastor, I should believe him. But the story keeps getting crazier.*

"I guess you could say," Alan continued slowly, "the stolen gem was stolen again."

After a few moments Scott replied, "What a shame. What a shame." He looked at Alan and reached over the counter to shake his hand. "Thanks for coming back. And thanks for keeping me informed about what's going on."

"Sure. I thought you ought to know. So, will you inform the International Jewelers Association that La Peregrina was thought to be found, but has been stolen again?"

"Yes, that'll be my next step," Scott assured him. "Let me know if you hear anything from the police."

"I will," Alan said as he turned from the counter. "I'll let you know."

Alan got into the car and sat there thinking. *I wasn't planning on telling him about the robbery. I guess it doesn't hurt that he knows. The Salem Police and Silverton Police are probably in communication. The Marion County Sheriff's Office is probably involved as well. It does seem strange that if Scott reported his suspicions to the Salem Police that they didn't come looking for the pearl that afternoon or evening. Instead, two criminals came to the door. Oh well, maybe Scott didn't actually report it to the police until the following day.*

As soon as Alan left the store, Scott called the Silverton Police Department to inquire. "I'm a jeweler in Salem. Can you tell me if my customer, Alan Johnson, was robbed recently?"

"We can't give out any specific information because there is an on-going investigation. But to answer your question: Yes, a robbery report has been filed."

Apparently, that part of Alan's story was true. He returned to his work, re-setting the gems on a ring he had been working on. He felt a little guilty about lying. He had not filed a report with the Salem Police because he had simply forgotten. The other fact Scott had forgotten was the conversation with another jeweler the previous afternoon about having La Peregrina in his store, and the guy from Silverton who brought it in. What jeweler wouldn't be excited about seeing that famous gem?

Pastor Alan Johnson was somewhat relieved the pearl was gone. He and Traci no longer had to worry about where to keep it, or where to take it, or how much it was worth. However, there was still one question gnawing at his mind. Who was the rightful owner? Surely the police would have access to information, such as when was it stolen? And who were the rightful owners?

The following week, on his grocery trip to Salem, he stopped at the jewelry store and talked to Scott again. "I've been curious about that famous pearl that I had for a very short time. You said you researched and found it was La Peregrina, once owned by Elizabeth Taylor. Did your research show who the current rightful owner is?"

"No, it didn't give any names. I got the information from the International Jewelers Association which said the pearl went missing in June this year. It said: If found, report to the Association. No details about who owns it."

"Okay, I guess it's none of my business any more. I really don't need to know." Alan thanked Scott and left to go get groceries.

CHAPTER 8

THE GUN

The luggage handler at PDX was excited to see a gun case on the rack, waiting to be loaded onto Flight 515. DeMar told his partner he had to go to the restroom, and when his buddy turned his back, he picked up the case and took it into the restroom. Inside the stall, he picked the lock and removed the contents, the handgun which he expected to find, and a large shiny pearl which he wasn't expecting. He put the pearl in his pocket, tucked the gun inside his baggy shirt, and re-locked the gun case. He peeked out the door to make sure no one was watching and returned the gun case to the rack, ready for loading. Ten minutes later the case was put on the conveyor belt and lifted to the belly of Flight 515.

The gun was hidden in DeMar's locker most of the day. When it was time to quit, he tucked it again into his shirt and walked out to the parking garage. At home he snuck it into the house, told his wife Laticia he had a good day, and hid the gun and pearl under the bed.

That evening he phoned the guy who had approached him at the airport a month ago. "If you ever get hold of a gun you don't need, give me a call. I've got contacts with street people who will pay good money." Al was glad the anonymous stranger answered on the second ring.

"Yea, who is it?" the voice answered.

"This is DeMar. I work at the airport, and I've got a gun I think you can use."

"Meet me at Tiny's Bar & Grill at 9 pm. I'll be wearing a Mariner's cap. Don't let anyone see the gun." Click.

A couple of hours later DeMar nervously entered Tiny's and looked around. One guy at the bar was sitting alone and wearing a Mariner's cap. DeMar walked up to the bar and took a seat. The bartender came over and asked DeMar what he wanted. "Bud Light," DeMar replied and pulled out a $5.

The stranger didn't look at him but mumbled, "Hey, buddy, what's your name?"

"DeMar," he replied. The bartender returned, placed the beer in front of him, and picked up the $5 bill. "Keep the change," DeMar said as the bartender walked away.

"Listen carefully, DeMar. Unzip your jacket. Don't let anybody but me see the goods. Understand?"

"Yeah," DeMar responded, and slowly unzipped his jacket. He reached slowly into his coat and lifted the gun near the opening.

The stranger glanced at DeMar and then down into the jacket. "Hmm, Sig Sauer." He looked up at the ceiling then spoke again. "$50 cash."

DeMar knew it was worth several hundred, maybe five hundred. "That's ridiculous. I risked my job to get this baby," DeMar whispered angrily.

"$100 final offer. Take it or leave it."

"Deal," DeMar responded reluctantly. Below bar level the exchange took place. DeMar looked to make sure the $100 bill appeared legitimate, and tucked it into his pocket.

The stranger placed the gun on the bar, pulled a pair of handcuffs from his jacket and said, "You're under arrest." Another undercover officer stepped up on the other side of DeMar, showed him a badge, and recited his rights, as the first officer snapped the cuffs on DeMar's wrists.

DeMar had nothing but regret on the short ride to the Portland Police Department. He was charged with unlicensed sale of a weapon and unlawful possession, and walked to a nearby cell. The officers checked the serial number which had not yet been filed off. The gun wasn't registered in the Oregon state records, but a national search produced the name Chuck Haskell in New York State.

DeMar was allowed to call Laticia and tell her he wouldn't be home because he was in jail. "Don't worry, honey. I'm sure I'll be out in a day or two. You'd better call the airline first thing in the morning, and tell them I'm sick and can't come to work tomorrow. And would you call our attorney tomorrow and have him come down here? Oh . . . and tell the kids I love them."

The following day, Portland police called Chuck in New York, who was relieved to learn the gun had been recovered. They promised to return the handgun as soon as their paperwork was finished. Chuck asked if anything else was found with the gun; however, there was no mention of the pearl.

CHAPTER 9

ALAN'S CONSCIENCE

E ver since those two well-dressed thugs had entered his house, Alan could not release his anger. He and Traci had planned to take the pearl to the police station. He realized they shouldn't try to keep it. Now it was gone. But he felt it was partly his fault that it was not in the hands of the rightful, legal owner. He should have taken it to the police the day he found it. If only he had known its value. If only he had taken it to the police on the way home from the jewelers. If only, if only.

Driven partly by guilt, partly by anger, and partly by curiosity, he vowed he wouldn't give up. Traci urged him to just "let it go." But Alan was determined to do 'something' to help get the pearl back where it belonged. He didn't even know where that was! There were still several questions bouncing around in his brain, and he wanted some answers.

Make a list. Alan was good at making lists. He wrote down who he needed to talk to, in order to get each question answered. International

Jewelers Association? Do they have a website? Do the police have any recent information on who stole the pearl from us? Did Scott give our name and address to anyone else? Or just to the IJA? Who has access to IJA?

First on the list, the IJA. Yes, they have a website. Check it out. No tab listing stolen or missing jewelry. Click on CONTACT US. Automatic Question: What is your concern? Alan's answer: List of stolen or missing jewelry. Answer: Only available to registered jewelers.

Alan tried calling the phone number. Answer: List is only available to registered jewelers. Alan decided to try a risky maneuver. "This is Alan Johnson and I have La Peregrina." Surely that would get a response. Sure enough, a real person answered the phone.

"This is Alan Johnson in Silverton, Oregon, and I found La Peregrina."

"We're sorry, but according to our records, La Peregrina was in your possession for only a short time. It was reported stolen again. I can't tell you anything further." Dead end.

Second call on the list, Silverton Police Department. Make an appointment to visit with Sergeant Phillips. Done. Ask question: Do you have any further leads on who stole the pearl from our house? Answer: None, sorry. Question: Has the pearl turned up anywhere else? Answer: Not to our knowledge. Dead end.

Third call on the list, Sylvia with Bright Gem Insurance. "Hello Sylvia, this is Alan Johnson, the pastor who had possession of La Peregrina for a short time. As we told you, it was stolen from us on August 5th. I hope the pearl has been found and returned to its rightful owner."

"I'm sorry to say it has not been found," Sylvia replied.

"I am working with the police here in Silverton. Can you tell us who the true owner is?"

"No, as I've said before, the owner who has the pearl insured with us, asked to remain anonymous."

"Can I give you a message to give to them?" Alan implored.

"I suppose we could, but I don't see why that would be necessary."

"I'm a pastor. I had possession of their pearl. I just want to express my sympathy to them. May I please send a note or letter to your office and ask you to forward it to them?"

"I guess that would be all right. Is there anything else?" Sylvia was running out of patience.

"No, thank you very much. And good luck with your continued investigation," Alan concluded.

"Thank you, good-by." Sylvia hung up and hoped the pastor wouldn't send a letter.

Another dead end. One more person on his list. Scott, the jeweler. Alan dialed the store and asked for Scott. "Sorry to bother you, but if I come to the store this afternoon, may I have a few minutes to visit in your office?"

"No problem," Scott replied. "What time?"

"Is two o'clock okay?"

"Sure. See you then."

At two, Alan rattled the familiar bell above the door and entered the store. Scott was waiting for him. "C'mon in." They walked back to the small office.

"I am just so frustrated," Alan began. "And angry," he continued. "About being robbed."

"I don't blame you," Scott sympathized.

"I've been wracking my brain to see if there is anything I can do to track down the pearl, and get it back to the rightful owner."

Scott nodded in understanding.

"I understand you have access to the International Jewelers Association," Alan paused.

"Limited access. Mainly through their website."

"Do you have any idea what has happened in the search for the pearl? Or who the legal owner might be?"

"No, nothing like that," Scott answered.

"One other question is still bothering me. Will you please think carefully and be very honest with me?" Alan paused again. "Did you tell anyone . . anyone . . that I had the pearl?"

Scott thought a few moments. "Well, I suppose Darla knew. She's the one who greets people when they first come in. And she knew you wanted an appraisal."

"Is it okay if I talk to Darla about this?" Alan asked.

"I suppose. But I doubt that she told anyone. We have a confidentiality policy which all of our employees agree to observe."

"Okay, is there anyone else you might have told about the pearl?"

"Not that I can think of. Confidentiality, you know."

"Did you tell your wife?" Alan asked.

"I'm not married," Scott replied with a smile. "Not for a long time now."

"Weren't you excited when you found out La Peregrina was here in your store?"

"Of course. Wait a minute. I just remembered a conversation with Bud Parker at Fred Meyer Jewelers. I told him on the phone that you brought in a large pearl, and it turned out to be La Peregrina. I forgot about that conversation until just now. But he wouldn't tell anyone."

Alan took a deep breath of frustration and let it out. "Of course not."

After briefly questioning Darla, Alan was fairly confident she had not told anyone. And if she had talked about the big pearl she had seen, the word might have spread all over Salem, with no one really caring about Darla's big experience.

Another week had passed with nothing but dead ends. Alan kept wondering, *How did the thieves find out I had the pearl? And where is it now?* He sat down at his desk and started writing.

Dear Anonymous Owners of La Peregrina:

I am writing to express my sympathy for your loss. I understand another name for La Peregrina is The Wanderer, and that its history is a story of lost and founds. Now I am a part of that history as well. My wife and I have been happily retired and living in Silverton, Oregon, for the past eight years. I served as a Lutheran pastor for nearly forty years, and now do supply preaching for pastors on vacation here in the Willamette Valley. How we came into possession of the pearl is an incident even I find hard to believe.

I was mowing our lawn about a month ago, when suddenly this stone dropped on my lawn. I looked up to see a large raven flying overhead. I picked up the stone and didn't realize until after taking it to a jeweler, that it was a rare and precious pearl known as La Peregrina. I also learned from the jeweler that it had been reported lost or stolen by the International Jewelers Association who would not reveal the legal owners who wished to remain anonymous.

Unfortunately, before I could take the pearl to the police, two armed men came to our door and demanded the gem. I had no choice but to give it to them. My wife and I were upset and extremely shaken by the robbery. I have no idea how those men knew we had the pearl. I do sincerely regret not taking it to the police the day I found it.

We were also contacted by Sylvia, a representative of Bright Gem Insurance, who came to our home for an interview. We planned to return the pearl to her. However, the robbery took place the evening before our appointment with her. We gave her all the information we could, and I'm sure you have been notified by her.

We are thankful that Sylvia agreed to forward this letter to you, so that you may remain anonymous. I simply wanted to express our sadness, and our apology for your continued loss. We share in just a small way, your frustration and sadness.

Most sincerely, Alan and Traci Johnson

CHAPTER 10

A CALL FROM JEANINE

A lan and Traci didn't really expect a reply from the anonymous owners of La Peregrina. The phone call came on a Sunday as they were returning home from church. As they got out of the car in their garage, they heard their phone ringing on the desk in the kitchen. Alan ran into the house and grabbed the phone. "Hello?"

"Oh, hello. This is Jeanine Woodburn. I hope I'm not calling at a bad time."

"No, my wife and I just got home from church." Alan waited, wondering *Who is Jeanine Woodburn?*

"My parents are Mark and Janet Woodburn from Glendale, California. They received the nice letter you wrote about a week ago."

"The letter about the pearl?"

"Yes, they're the anonymous owners of La Peregrina, and they asked me to call you and thank you for writing and expressing your concern."

"Thank you for calling. Can you hold for just a minute? My wife is coming in from the garage." Alan put his hand over the receiver and whispered to Traci, "This is the real owner of the pearl. She's calling to thank us for the letter I wrote." Traci nodded understanding.

Alan spoke again into the phone, "I'm sorry; what did you say your name was?" He pressed the button for speaker phone so Traci could listen in.

"Jeanine Woodburn. And my parents are Mark and Janet. My dad is a Hollywood entrepreneur. He bought the pearl for my mom several years ago at an auction in New York. He gave it to her for Christmas in 2011."

"Oh, how tender! As I said in my letter, we feel so badly about this whole situation. My wife and I fell in love with La Peregrina during the few weeks we had it. I can't imagine how hard this is for your parents."

"The reason I'm calling, instead of them making the call, is this. Do you have a minute?"

"Sure, no hurry," Alan replied.

"A couple of months ago, a friend of mine got married in Portland. She asked me to be one of her attendants, so my parents flew up from Los Angeles for the wedding. My mom was wearing La Peregrina, and at the reception I told her how much I had always admired it. She gave me a hug. Then she told me, she and dad had decided it would be a wedding gift to me when I got married! Can you believe it? I was so excited. I had just witnessed my best friend saying her vows. Now I pictured myself saying my vows with La Peregrina lying against my wedding dress."

Alan and Traci smiled at each other. "Now we feel doubly sad, knowing the necklace would have been yours."

"Actually, I'm enjoying my work in Phoenix, and I'm not planning on getting married in the near future."

"Did you enjoy your time in Portland?" Alan asked.

"Yes, very much. Up until the reception ended with my mom being attacked. Some guy just ran up to them in the parking lot and pulled the pearl off her necklace."

"Was she hurt in the attack?"

"Not physically, just emotionally."

"We've been wondering how the pearl was lost by its legal owner; now we know. How terrible to have it stolen like that! Is there anything more we can do?" Alan asked.

"Not really," Jeanine replied. "Just let us know if you learn anything more about its whereabouts."

"We certainly will."

"Let me give you my number in Phoenix."

"Thank you, Jeanine. And thank you for calling."

Alan hung up the phone and wrote down the names, Jeanine Woodburn. Mark and Janet Woodburn, Glendale, CA. "Let's keep this to ourselves." Traci nodded in agreement.

CHAPTER 11

WHERE IS LA PEREGRINA?

D eMar, the airline employee who had removed the gun and the pearl from the locked case, sat in his cell with his head in his hands. He was glad it was morning. He had not enjoyed his night in the Portland jail cell. His cellmate was an obnoxious young creep, covered with tattoos, and he smelled horrible. Fortunately, DeMar's attorney appeared about 10 am, and after filling out the paperwork, and signing numerous forms, DeMar was released until his court date. He hoped he could continue working until then. He knew he would probably lose his job when the airlines learned he had been convicted of theft. He hoped his wife had called the airlines to tell them he was sick and couldn't come to work today.

Upon arriving home, Laticia was extremely upset. She couldn't believe he had spent the night in jail, and she wanted to know the whole story. He explained the best he could, telling her about the locked gun case and his hopes to sell the gun.

"How could you?" was her angry response. After each part of the story she repeated, "How could you?" Finally, she turned away and went into the bedroom. "Leave me alone," she said as she closed the door behind her.

DeMar lay down on the sofa. He wanted to check under the bed to see if the pearl was still there. That would have to wait until later. He laid on the sofa reviewing the past several days. He felt nothing but regret until he finally dozed off.

That evening at the dinner table, there was very little conversation. "I'm really sorry," was all DeMar could think of. Laticia just nodded.

The next morning DeMar dressed and headed for the airport. When he got into the terminal, he met a few of the other employees. He faked a couple of coughs and said, "I'm feeling a lot better today." Loading baggage onto the plane felt refreshing. Sure, it was tiring, tossing bag after bag onto the conveyor. Still, it was a great job and it paid well. *I'm actually going to miss this,* he thought to himself.

As the day went on, he considered his options with the pearl. Give it to the police was the most obvious. But how could he do that without being accused of stealing the pearl as well as the gun? By the time he got home he knew what he would do. As soon as they finished eating dinner, DeMar told his wife he had an errand to run. And he promised not to get into trouble this time! He went into the bedroom and dug the pearl out from under the bed. He grabbed a paper bag from the kitchen drawer, went out to the garage, and got into the car, and put the pearl into the bag.

DeMar drove to the Port of Portland, Property Division, on Airport Way. He had driven past the building every day on his way to work. DeMar parked close to the front door, about thirty feet away.

He picked up the bag from the front seat and got out of the car. He pulled his cap down over his eyes as he walked casually toward the office. When he reached the door, he glanced around to see that no one was watching. He slipped quietly into the foyer. To his right was a locked door and a double thick glass window with a microphone for talking with staff after normal hours. There were lights on inside the office, and the foyer was well-lit also. He set the bag in front of the door. He knocked three times on the door, then quickly exited the building.

He didn't run to the car but walked very quickly. He put the key in the ignition, started the car, glanced in the rear-view mirror, and was relieved to see no one coming out of the station. At least the pearl was no longer in his possession.

CHAPTER 12

BACK TO ALAN

The officers in the Property Division glanced at the screen to see who had knocked. The man was leaving through the door. They could see a small bag in front of the office door. They opened the door carefully and picked up the bag. Inside was a large pearl, nothing else. A check of online crime reports showed a report of a pearl being stolen in downtown Portland back in June, and a more recent report of a robbery in Silverton, apparently the same large pearl! Now it was here in northeast Portland, secure in the Property Division.

The last report gave the owner's name as Alan Johnson, and listed his address and phone number in Silverton. While one officer photographed the pearl and tagged it with an official number, another officer called the number in California. There was no answer, so he called the number in Silverton.

Alan got up from the sofa in the living room and hurried into the kitchen to see if it was another robo-call. The screen said PDX POLICE. Alan picked it up. "Hello."

"Yes, we're calling from the Port of Portland Police Department. This is the Property Division in northeast Portland. Is this Alan Johnson?"

"Yes, I'm Alan."

"We are calling to report that a stolen item has just been dropped off here at this office, and it matches the description of the item stolen from your home a couple of weeks ago." He was testing to see if this Alan Johnson knew what "item" he was talking about.

"You've got the pearl!" Alan nearly screamed. "You've got La Peregrina?"

"We believe it is the same pearl. It is very large, and pear-shaped."

"Oh my gosh! That's wonderful news!" Alan turned and shouted into the living room, "Traci, they've found the pearl!" Alan didn't bother explaining that the pearl should actually be returned to the Woodburn's in Glendale. He was still trying to keep the true owners anonymous.

"As soon as we finish the paper work here," the officer continued, "we'll take the pearl to the Silverton Police Station and have the officer in charge there, bring it to your home."

"Oh, thank God! I am so glad the pearl's been found. Thank you for calling."

As soon as the police hung up, he dialed Jeanine's number in Phoenix.

"Hi, Jeanine. This is Alan Johnson. I've got some good news. They've found the pearl!"

All Alan heard was a screech. Then Jeanine replied, "Oh my god! That's wonderful! Where is it?"

"It's in the hands of the police here in Portland. I just got a phone call a few minutes ago."

"That's wonderful news. Whatever you do, please don't give them my name or number, or my parents' names."

"I haven't. And I won't. I guess I'll just let them return it to me, and we'll pretend it's ours."

"And I'll talk to my folks and ask how they want it returned. We'll stay in touch. Thank you so much for calling."

The following morning, Alan dialed Scott's office at the jewelry store. The answering machine gave him the message: If you have an urgent need, call my cell phone 503-602-1791. Alan dialed again. "Scott, I just got some great news. The Portland Police have the pearl."

"That is great news," Scott replied. "I'll notify the International Jewelers Association that it's been recovered."

"And I'm calling Sylvia," Alan responded. "She's the investigator from Bright Gem, the company that insured the pearl. It will finally be back in the hands of the rightful owner."

"Who's that?" Scott asked.

"Can't say," Alan replied. "They want to remain anonymous. I'll see to it that the pearl gets back to them as quickly as possible."

Scott had a feeling that Alan knew, but wouldn't tell. "Thanks for calling," Scott said. As soon as he hung up, Scott got online and entered the news for the IJA website:

> LA PEREGRINA HAS BEEN FOUND
> The pearl is back in the possession of retired pastor
> Alan Johnson in Silverton, Oregon. It will soon be
> in the hands of the legal owners who wish to remain
> anonymous.

The news traveled quickly. On the east coast, the jeweler who was a close friend of Leonardo Dantoni, saw the posting on the International Jewelers Association website. Within minutes he was on the phone to Dantoni. "The pearl's been found in Oregon. I don't have any details about its recovery, but it is back in the possession of the retired pastor, Alan Johnson, in Silverton."

"Thanks for the call," Dantoni responded. "I'll get right on it."

A phone call to Dale at his apartment in the Bronx was all it took to put things in motion. "Dale, the pearl is back in possession of that pastor. Don't ask me how it got there. All I know is he's got it. But he may not have it for long, so get moving. I want that pearl."

"Right, boss. I'll be in touch with Chuck, and we'll be back with the pearl before you can say Hell Yes."

"And don't screw it up this time."

Late that night, Chuck and Dale were on a plane heading for Portland. Again.

CHAPTER 13

CRUNCH TIME AT SILVERTON GULCH

A s Dale and Chuck drove their rental car from the airport to the Benson Hotel, they discussed the plan of attack. "We can't just walk up to the front door like we did last time," Dale began.

"Yeah, they'd recognize us for sure," Chuck replied. The entrance ramp onto the Banfield Freeway was clear, so Dale sped up to merge on I-84. "Do you suppose they'd open up if they saw my gun?" Chuck asked.

"Nah, they'd probably run for the phone and hit 9-1-1." Dale pulled into the middle lane to pass a motor home heading toward I-5. "Maybe we should do some surveillance this time and get to know when they're home and when they go out."

Chuck unlocked the gun case, tucked the Sig Sauer into his underarm holster, and placed the case on the floor in back. "Maybe break in the house when they're out shopping?"

"Yea, that might work," Dale replied. "Do you remember if they had a security system or cameras?"

"No, I don't remember. It was just so easy last time. That stupid pastor just opened the door."

"It won't be as easy this time. I can guarantee that." Dale drove past Lloyd Center, merged onto I-5 South and took the first exit ramp to the Morrison Bridge. In a matter of minutes, they were in the parking garage at the Benson, and unloading their suitcases. "Let's check out of here tomorrow," Dale offered. "We'll have to stay in Silverton to keep an eye on the Johnson's."

* * *

Alan and Traci were glad the pearl was in "police custody." They agreed they didn't want it back in their house until they knew exactly how and when they would return it to the Woodburn's. "Why don't we just put it in a box and send it FedEx?" Alan suggested.

Traci laughed. "Great idea! But we should insure it for at least a hundred dollars," Traci responded. Alan laughed.

"Maybe Jeanine will fly up here from Phoenix," Traci pondered. "She could get La Peregrina at the police station and fly down to L.A. to return it to her parents."

"Or maybe her parents will fly up to Portland to retrieve it," Alan suggested as another possibility.

"Let's call the Silverton Police and ask if they'll keep it safe until we settle on a plan."

"I think that's a great idea," Alan agreed. "Do you want to call them? Or should I?"

"You do it," Traci said emphatically.

The Silverton Police Chief spoke to Alan, "We would be happy to keep La Peregrina locked up at the station for the time being. Let us know when you want it. We won't turn it over to anyone except you. Our records indicate that you are the owner."

"That's fine," Alan replied. "We'll be in touch."

On Wednesday, Jeanine called back. "I've talked with my parents, and they are so grateful to both of you. I know they're excited to see La Peregrina. My dad said the necklace is polished and waiting."

"Will they be coming to Silverton? Or will you?" Alan asked.

"Oh, no!" Jeanine replied. "They want you to come to Glendale! They said they'd even take you to Disneyland, or anywhere else you'd like to visit. Have you ever been to Catalina?"

"Wow! That's a nice offer. We weren't expecting anything like that!"

"They'll pay for your flight. And they said they'll meet you at LAX. They have a limo so you can all ride back together to Glendale."

"That is so generous of them. I'll talk with Traci and see what she thinks. I have a hunch she'll be very excited."

"You go ahead and book the flight," Jeanine said. "Let me know what day and what flight you'll be on, and I'll pass the information to my parents. Mark and Janet are excited to meet you. And, of course, you'll be reimbursed for any and all expenses."

Traci was indeed excited to hear about the invitation to fly to L.A. and to meet the Woodburn's. They reviewed their calendar and started making plans.

Chuck and Dale were getting nervous. The Johnson's were retired, and it seemed they never left the house. They were pleased to see there were no security cameras on the house, but a sign near the front door indicated an inside security alarm of some kind. On Thursday morning, they observed the garage door opening, and Traci backing out of the garage. Dale noted Alan and Traci had only one car. They followed her at a safe distance and discovered she was driving to the gym for her daily exercise routine. Alan was home alone. Maybe that would be the time to strike. They decided to observe for another day or two before attempting a break-in.

When Traci returned from the gym, the garage door opened, and this time Dale observed the circuit breaker box inside the garage. Knowing where that was located might come in handy. The rest of the day passed without either Alan or Traci leaving the house. At 7:15 pm Dale and Chuck left to get something to eat, then went back to the Silverton Inn tired and bored.

Friday morning, they ate an early breakfast and were parked on the street when the garage door opened. Traci was by herself. They assumed she was heading for the gym again. This time she was on her way to the beauty shop for her hair appointment. Getting her hair done once a week was the one treat she gave herself. It lifted her spirits and helped her feel good to be "out and about." Dale followed her down Main Street, and this time, instead of parking at the gym, she turned into the parking lot at Visions Beauty Salon. Again, they waited until she came out and followed her again, this time to the bank.

"Oh, no!" Dale nearly screamed. "What if she's taking the pearl and putting it in a deposit box?"

"Oh, shit!" Chuck replied. "If that's the case, we're screwed." Traci came out in just a few minutes, and Chuck and Dale followed her home.

Friday was also their "date night." Ever since they retired, Traci and Alan had a date on Friday night, going out for dinner to a nice restaurant in Salem or Silverton. Sometimes they combined some shopping at Kohl's or Macy's. And when they returned home, it was movie night. They weren't great fans of the new movies, but enjoyed one of their old favorites once a week.

Chuck and Dale were watching from their car when Alan and Traci pulled out at 4:30 to go to dinner. Again, they followed from a distance to see where they were going. Silverton Road is the most direct highway to Salem, about 12 miles away. After following them for two or three miles, Dale pulled off at the Brush Creek Playhouse, and turned around in the parking lot. He headed back into town and asked Chuck, "Are you ready?"

"Let's do it," Chuck replied.

Again, they parked on the street and put on their Covid masks, more to hide their faces than to prevent the spread of disease. They walked up the Johnson's driveway, circled the garage, and approached the back garage door. It was locked. They looked around and saw no one watching, so Chuck lifted his leg and gave the door handle a hard kick. The door cracked, but the lock held. He kicked it again, and this time the door broke loose, and they were in. Dale went immediately to the circuit panel and switched off every circuit breaker. From the garage they entered the kitchen. So far, no alarm sounded. They headed to the bedroom where the pearl had been before.

Dale pulled open Traci's dresser drawer, but it wasn't there. Drawer by drawer, the same thing. No pearl. "Check that other dresser," he said to Chuck, as he moved to the closet. Dale and Chuck continued searching, pulling out drawer by drawer, dumping the contents, and shelf by shelf, pushing everything on the floor. "Shit!" Dale yelled.

"I'll go through the kitchen," Chuck offered. "Why don't you check the other bedroom?" Finally, they met in the living room, and went through the furniture there. Still nothing.

"Wait a minute," Dale looked at Chuck, "we didn't check the bathrooms." One headed into the master bathroom; the other went to the bathroom off the hall. Still nothing.

Back in the kitchen they stood staring at each other. "Doesn't appear to be here," Chuck said.

Dale raised his arms in frustration. "Maybe Traci put it in the deposit box at the bank."

"Do you think they might have left it with the police?" Chuck asked, shrugging his shoulders.

"I suppose that's a possibility too," Dale replied. "Let's get out of here."

They didn't bother to turn on the electricity, just walked out to their car and drove to the motel.

When Alan and Traci returned, they couldn't understand why the garage door opener wouldn't work. They parked in front of the garage and used their key to let themselves in the front door. Once in the living room, they nearly fainted. The house was a disaster. And they knew why. Alan went into the garage and flipped the breakers. At least they had light. And the TV worked. Although they didn't feel like watching a movie.

Alan picked up the phone and called the police. "We want to report a break-in at our home," Alan began.

"We'll send someone right away," the woman replied. "What is your address?"

Alan and Traci waited for the officer to arrive, then showed him the damage. He wrote up the report and expressed his condolences. They spent the rest of the evening cleaning up the mess as best they could.

CHAPTER 14

WE NEED A PLAN

⸺⬦⸺

The Johnson's were shaken again, frightened, and still vulnerable.
"Should we buy a gun?" Traci asked.

"I've thought about that too, but I'm not comfortable with the idea," Alan replied. "They have a lot more experience with weapons than we do. I don't like the idea of a stand-off or worse yet, a shoot-out."

"I kinda feel the same way," Traci nodded with understanding. "I never have liked guns."

"I'll have to give this a lot of thought," Alan continued. "We'll be leaving next week for California. We have to pick up La Peregrina at the police station, carry it with us to the airport, move through check-in, and board the plane. We'll be so darn vulnerable."

"I don't want to think about it," Traci answered.

"We need a plan," Alan replied. "I'll give it some thought."

"You're good at planning. I'll just pray for you," Traci said sweetly.

"Thanks, honey."

Chuck and Dale needed a plan too. It was obvious the pearl was not at the house. It had to be in the bank safe, or at the police department. "Let's keep a log of their activities," Dale suggested.

"You mean like writing notes every day about what they're doin' and where they're goin'?"

"That's exactly what I mean," Dale affirmed. "You're good with the binoculars, so you keep an eye on the house and garage. I'll write the notes when you see them leaving. When we follow them to the gym or grocery store, we'll write it down."

"What if they go to the bank?" Chuck asked. "Or what if they go to the police station?"

Dale thought a minute, "Good questions. I hope we'll be able to see something that indicates they are picking up the pearl. Maybe they'll have a special case for it, like you do for your gun."

For the rest of the week, Chip and Dale continued their stakeout, taking notes on the Johnson's activities.

Alan woke up one morning excited about his ideas. He hoped it wouldn't be needed, but he had a plan. He shared the ideas with Traci, and she agreed to help if necessary. His first phone call was to Jeanine Woodburn in Phoenix. After talking with Jeanine, Alan made the plane reservations to fly to Los Angeles to return La Peregrina. The flight was Alaska Airlines, flight 3331, leaving PDX at 12:50 pm on Tuesday the 27th.

Next, he called Scott and asked for help. "I need a fake pearl," Alan told him. "Can you make an imitation La Peregrina?"

"Sure," Scott answered, "when do you need it?"

"We're leaving town next Tuesday. Can I pick it up on Monday? I'll be glad to pay you for it."

"No problem. I'll have it ready."

The next thing he needed was his old briefcase. It had a cheap lock, and fortunately, Alan found the key for it in one of his dresser drawers.

He called Sergeant Phillips at the Silverton Police Station and asked if he could pick up the pearl.

"When do you want it?" Phillips asked.

"Next Tuesday morning."

"There will be some paper work to fill out, but I'll plan to be here to help you with that," the Sergeant added.

"I really appreciate you keeping it locked up these past couple of weeks. I'm glad it wasn't at our home when the thieves broke in."

"You bet. I'm glad it was here. And I'm glad no one was hurt. Just a heck of a mess as I recall."

"Thanks, Sergeant. See you on Tuesday."

There was one more scary part which Traci would not appreciate. With all the pieces in place, it was time to discuss it with her. He helped with the dishes after dinner. They went into the living room.

"Before we pack our suitcases, I've got something I need to discuss with you," Alan started the conversation.

Sensing his seriousness, Traci asked, "Is it part of your plan?"

"Yes," Alan acknowledged. "As I said before, I hope we don't need it, but here it is. You know I asked our jeweler friend, Scott, to make an imitation of La Peregrina. If, by some chance, the thieves make another attempt to rob us, it will probably be on our way to the airport."

Traci grimaced.

"Tomorrow morning, we'll go to the police station to pick up La Peregrina, I'll take the old briefcase in with me. I'll put the real pearl in my pocket, and the fake pearl will be in the briefcase when I go in and when I come out. I'll carefully lay the briefcase on the back seat just in case those thieves are watching us. Naturally, they'll think I picked up the real pearl and locked it in the briefcase for our trip."

"That's a cool plan," Traci nodded, "but when do you think they'll attempt to rob us? On the way to the police station? On the way to the airport? Or at the airport?"

"I don't know," Alan answered honestly. "Never, I hope."

Traci thought for a minute. "Now I'm feeling scared and vulnerable again."

"Yeah, I know," Alan replied, "but here's what we need to do. The brief case will be in the back seat of the car. I'll give it to them when they demand it. But . . . I don't want it to be too easy. We've got to be scared and frightened and upset and angry that they have assaulted us again."

"Being frightened won't be hard for me," Traci confessed. "What if something goes wrong?"

"Well, that's where we hope the plan is successful. They'll take the briefcase and scram. Maybe that's where our faith has to take over. I trust God more than I trust those creeps."

"Like I said before, I'll just keep praying." Traci gave Alan a hug. "Let's get packing!" Traci headed to the bedroom while Alan pulled the suitcases out of the closet.

Alan and Traci were awake early Tuesday morning. "I'm excited to meet the Woodburn's," Traci said, as she tucked her makeup into her suitcase. "I'm nervous about the pearl."

"Me too," Alan agreed. "But let's try to focus on the fun we'll have in Los Angeles, and not on what MIGHT happen before we get there."

Tuesday morning, Chuck and Dale began their usual surveillance routine, parking up the block from the Johnson's. "I suppose Traci will head for the gym about 9 or 9:30 like she usually does," Dale commented as he pulled out his notebook. They waited. But Traci didn't leave for the gym. At 10:05 the garage door went up, and Chuck raised his binoculars.

"Oh, oh," he said to Dale. "Alan is loading two suitcases into the trunk."

"Suitcases!" Dale nearly shouted. "They must be going somewhere."

"And it looks like a briefcase that he just put on the back seat," Chuck replied.

In a few minutes Traci came out and climbed into the front seat and put on her seat belt while Alan got into the driver's seat. They backed out and lowered the garage door. Dale started their car to follow the Johnson's. Hanging back about a block, they followed them down Main

Street, and then turned right on Water Street downtown. After a few blocks, Alan pulled to the curb and parked in front of the Silverton Police Station.

"Jesus, do you suppose he's getting the pearl?" Chuck asked. They pulled over and watched, as Alan got out, opened the back door, and took the briefcase into the police station. Chuck and Dale waited anxiously.

"You're darn right!" Dale replied. "Traci's just sitting in the car waiting."

Five minutes later, Alan came out with the briefcase, and put it again into the back seat. He started the car and drove off. North up the hill, past their church, out of town on highway 213. So far, so good. They had not seen the car that was following them or they'd have been really, really nervous.

Chuck and Dale followed. "Now where are they going?" Chuck asked.

CHAPTER 15

AT TACO TIME

As they followed Alan and Traci north on highway 213, Dale started pointing at the glove compartment. "Chuck, get the map out. Where does highway 213 take us?"

Chuck fumbled with the map and finally answered, "We're heading toward a town called Molalla. Then it goes to Oregon City near Portland, then Interstate 205."

"Well, shit! Of course. And Interstate 205 takes them to the airport," Dale replied. "They stopped at the police station to get the pearl! And now they're flying somewhere to return it. Shit yeah!"

"Hey, we oughta stop'em before they get to the airport," Chuck replied.

"Darn right!" Dale answered. He thought for a minute or two. "Probably before they get on the interstate. The less cars and people around, the better."

"Just pass 'em, cut 'em off, and drive 'em off the road into a ditch," Chuck responded.

"Yeah, that might work. Or they might crash into us and send us into a ditch," Dale replied.

"You're driving. What are you gonna do?"

"We'll play it smart and watch for the right opportunity," Dale answered. "Make sure you've got your gun ready."

It took about twenty minutes to reach Molalla. "I know it's too early for lunch, but I'm getting hungry," Alan said as they approached the town. "Maybe it's just my nerves."

"Pull off and get yourself a taco," Traci suggested. As the Safeway and Taco Time came into view, Alan turned on his turn signal and pulled in. He drove around the restaurant and got into the drive-up line to order.

Dale pulled into the parking lot and drove toward the Safeway store, then turned back toward Taco Time. "I think this is it," he said to Chuck. He pulled into a diagonal parking space where they could watch the Johnsons.

In a minute or two Alan pulled up to the window to get his taco. Traci didn't want anything.

Dale backed out of his parking place and pulled in front of Alan as he was leaving the window. Dale blocked the Johnson's car and put his car in Park. He and Chuck jumped out. Dale went to Alan's door; Chuck walked to the passenger side, pulled his gun, and pointed it at Traci. "Don't do anything stupid," Dale said. "You don't want a dead wife, do you? Just hand us the briefcase from the back seat."

"No, no, please?" Alan begged.

Chuck cocked the gun. "The briefcase," Dale repeated.

"Okay, okay, okay," Alan stuttered as he reached back and retrieved the case. He wasn't *acting* scared; he *was* scared. Alan handed it out through the window.

Dale laid it on top of the car above Alan's head, and used his pocket knife to pry open the lock. The pearl was there, bright and shiny. He shut the case, looked at Chuck and said, "We got it. Let's go." They walked back to their car, got in, backed up, and drove away. At the intersection, they took a right on highway 211 and drove toward I-5. Dale thought it would be better to take a different route back to Silverton, in case Alan called the police.

Alan didn't call the police. The thieves had a fake pearl. He and Traci stopped in the Safeway parking lot for a minute just to calm down. Then continued on their way to the airport. His plan had worked. At least they hoped it had. They wouldn't really be able to relax until they got on board Flight 3331.

Dale and Chuck returned to their room at the Silverton Inn. They opened the briefcase again and pumped their fists in the air. "All right!" They could hardly wait to get back to New York. Dantoni would be pleased. And the money, ah, the money! They took the pearl into the bathroom where the light was much better to admire their prize. It didn't seem as bright as they remembered, or as heavy. Chuck picked it up and tapped it gently on the sink ledge. It broke in his hand and crumbled into half a dozen pieces. "Goddammit! We've been had!" he screamed.

CHAPTER 16

CELEBRATION

A lan and Traci dragged their suitcases through the check-in line. At the counter Alan dropped La Peregrina into the corner of his bag which had been the more convenient. As they walked toward security, Alan realized it was good the pearl wasn't in his pocket. It might have gone through x-ray without any questions. But someone might have asked, "What is THAT?" On to Concourse B, Gate 6. And now the only carry-on was Traci's purse. Alan smiled when he thought about his old briefcase. *Good job, old boy. It was either carry the fake pearl, or go to Goodwill.* It had done its job. As they sat, waiting to board, Alan pictured the thieves when they discovered the pearl was a fake. A big smile broke across his face.

Once in the cabin, Alan and Traci fastened their seat belts and exchanged another kiss. Both took a deep breath, held each other's hand, closed their eyes, and listened as the flight attendant gave instructions. In a couple of hours, they were roused from their nap,

"We are beginning our descent into Los Angeles. Please make sure your seatbelts are fastened and all your belongings securely stowed."

Inside the terminal, as they headed for baggage claim, a young woman was holding a hand-printed sign: ALAN and TRACI. They approached her and asked, "Are you Jeanine?" She dropped the sign to her side and with the other arm reached out to give Traci a hug.

"Yes, I am," she replied. "It's so great to finally meet you in person."

"And we're glad to meet you!" Alan replied, as she gave him a hug with her free arm.

"We'll get your luggage downstairs," she said. "Then I'll call our limo."

Waiting for their bags to come down the turn-style, Traci began talking about their narrow escape in Molalla. Alan pulled the bags from the conveyor, and they headed outside. A shiny black limousine pulled up to the curb. Jeanine opened the door and ushered them inside. Alan was amazed how spacious it felt as he stepped in. There to greet them, sat Mark and Janet Woodburn.

"Welcome to LA!" Mark said as Alan and Traci took seats across from the Woodburn's. Jeanine sat next to her mom. As the limo pulled away from the airport, Mark reached into the cooler and pulled out a bottle of champagne. He raised the bottle and popped the cork. "Here's to the return of La Peregrina!" He poured a moderate amount into the plastic cups and passed them to Traci and Alan, to Jeanine and Janet. He raised his own cup and announced, "Let the celebration begin!"

After a sip or two of champagne, Janet asked about their trip. Before Traci or Alan could reply, Jeanine interrupted, "O my gosh! They were nearly robbed again on the way to the airport in Portland!"

"My Lord, what happened?" Janet asked.

"The same thieves that came to our home confronted us again," Traci responded. "We had pulled into a Taco Time in the little town of Molalla. They drove up in front of us at the drive-through window, pointed a gun at me, and demanded the pearl!"

"Oh, NO!" replied Janet. "Did you give it to them?"

"No, we didn't," Traci answered, smiling. "Alan had this wonderful plan. He had a fake pearl made, which he put in an old briefcase on the back seat. He handed them the briefcase and they took off with the fake pearl. We were so relieved!"

"That's amazing!" Mark replied. "Way to outsmart those darn thieves!"

"And that reminds me," Alan responded, "I had the real pearl in my pocket, and now it's in my suitcase. We'll present it to you as soon as we arrive at your home."

With traffic on 405 and the Ventura Freeway it took over an hour to get to Glendale. The Woodburn estate, when they finally arrived, was magnificent. That evening they enjoyed a sumptuous dinner prepared by the resident chef. Once the salads were placed on the table, and the wine was poured, Alan pulled the pearl from his pocket. "Sorry, there's no fancy wrapping," he said, as he handed the pearl to Janet.

"Under the circumstances, fancy wrapping could hardly be expected," Janet replied. "We're just so happy to see La Peregrina!" Janet gushed as she held it up in the light of the chandelier. "It seems even larger than I remember!"

"Let me propose another toast," Mark began. "Here's to a courageous couple, and to the return of the Wanderer." Mark lifted his wine glass, and was joined by the others. "We will have that pearl back on the necklace in a matter of days. I've already spoken with our jeweler."

After dinner, Mark asked Alan and Traci to follow him upstairs. There was something he wanted to show them. He and Janet led them into their bedroom suite. They walked past the king size bed and into an adjacent dressing room. Mark unlocked and opened a large wardrobe door, reached inside, and lifted down a necklace display bust holding the most magnificent necklace the Johnsons had ever seen. "Behold the Cartier necklace!" Mark announced. He placed it carefully on the dressing table and turned on the makeup lights.

Alan and Traci stood speechless, staring at the diamonds and rubies and pearls. Finally, Traci gasped, "That is the most beautiful necklace I have ever seen in my entire life!"

Mark put his arm around Janet. "I bought that for Janet from the Elizabeth Taylor collection after she passed away."

Janet smiled as she looked up at Mark. Then she turned to Traci and Alan. "Thank you so much for bringing La Peregrina home again." Janet handed the pearl to Mark, and he held it at the base of the necklace.

"The jeweler said he would re-attach it and the necklace will be good as new." All four of them continued staring for another minute or two. "Why don't we go back downstairs and visit a little more? And maybe have some dessert," Mark added.

He placed the necklace and pearl back into the closet and locked the door.

They visited for several hours talking about their families, places they had lived, and of course, the pearl. Jeanine excused herself early and headed upstairs to her room. An hour later, Janet escorted Traci and Alan to their guestroom.

"Tomorrow," Janet whispered, "we have a special day planned."

"What are we doing tomorrow?" Traci asked.

"It's a surprise!" Janet giggled. "Mark said I couldn't tell you until morning."

After a healthy breakfast and stout mug of espresso, Mark announced the plan. "Pack up your bags, and I hope you didn't forget your swimsuits. We're going to Santa Catalina!" Again, they all climbed into the limo, and headed for the harbor. Alan expected they would board a tour boat to take them to the island. But no, the limo pulled into a private marina and stopped. The driver got out and loaded all their bags onto a cart. Mark announced, "Follow me," and they proceeded down the gangplank and out to the Woodburn's yacht. Alan and Traci exchanged glances. They had never been exposed to this level of wealth and luxury.

Once on board, the diesel engines began to throb as they pulled away from the dock. The air was fresh and cool. "I've ordered the captain to take his time," Mark told them. "If you want to change into your swimsuits, we can enjoy the lounge chairs by the pool." As Alan and Traci changed clothes in their stateroom, they agreed this was a once-in-a-lifetime experience.

They enjoyed the day wandering about the streets on Catalina Island. They slept aboard the yacht that night. After breakfast, the engines rumbled again for the return to the mainland. Half way back to Marina del Rey, Traci hollered, "Alan, come here!" Together they leaned over the deck railing to watch several porpoises swimming along the bow of the boat.

Their five days in Glendale passed quickly with a trip to the Getty Art Museum and a full day at Disneyland. Alan and Traci were pleased with how comfortable they felt with Mark and Janet. Jeanine flew back to Phoenix after three days to return to work. The show she was working on was due to open October 5ᵗʰ.

One evening at dinner, Alan was reminiscing about his days of preaching every Sunday. "I was thinking about the parable of the lost coin. Remember how Jesus said, "A woman who had ten silver coins, lost one. She lit a lamp and swept the house, and searched diligently until she found it. And when she found it, she called together her friends and neighbors, saying 'Rejoice with me, for I have found the lost coin.'" Traci and I are so happy to be part of this celebration and the finding of La Peregrina."

"And Janet and I are so happy you and Traci have come to celebrate its return with us. I guess the legend of La Peregrina, the wanderer, continues. She disappears for a time, then reappears."

"Lost and found, lost and found," Alan added.

"Sad, then happy; sad, then happy!" Traci chimed in.

"Old friends and new friends," Janet added. "Here's to them all," she said as she raised her glass of wine. The others raised their glasses, nodded and smiled.

"La Peregrina continues her journey," Mark commented.

"And we had the privilege of being one chapter in that journey," Alan concluded.

"And tomorrow morning we'll take you two back to the airport." Janet pretended to wipe a tear from her eye.

The following evening, Alan and Traci were home in Silverton. "We may not be millionaires," Traci commented, "but we have a beautiful home, and each other."

"And sometimes it's nice to have millionaire friends," Alan laughed.

Traci nodded in agreement and replied, "Now empty those suitcases, and bring the dirty laundry in here so I can start the wash machine."

*   *   *

Dale and Chuck decided not to return to New York. They thought Portland might have possibilities. They rented a small apartment in the Lents neighborhood.

The following spring, Junior and June celebrated the arrival of three baby ravens in their nest at Silver Falls State Park.

INVASIVE SPECIES

A Long Short Story by

JIM BORNZIN

ADVENTURE FICTION – MYSTERY

INVASIVE SPECIES is a fun, easy-to-read short story or novella, inspired by a house plant given to the author by a friend. The author was in a bad mood and began to wonder, *what if the plant is making me grouchy?* In this novella, Alan and Traci return from a trip to Madagascar with a packet of seeds, which Traci plants and nurtures, never suspecting the danger lurking in this **invasive species.**

According to Wikipedia: An invasive species is an introduced organism that becomes overpopulated and harms its new environment. Although most introduced species are neutral or beneficial with respect to other species, invasive species adversely affect habitats and bioregions, causing ecological, environmental, and/or economic damage.

SILVERTON MYSTERIES features fictional tales from the life of Pastor Alan Johnson and his wife Traci. Expecting to live a "normal life" in the small, quiet town of Silverton, Oregon, they are little prepared for the unexpected and unbelievable, and sometimes unwanted events that ensue.

CHAPTER 1

SHE LOVES HER PLANTS

"THESE PLANTS ARE DRIVING ME CRAZY!" Alan had just returned from the public library with a spy novel he was anxious to read. He headed for his favorite spot on a sunny spring afternoon, the bay window seat soaked in sunshine. What he found was a ledge, newly arranged with his wife's potted house plants.

"Honey, the plants need the sunlight," Traci responded, fully believing that should be enough of an explanation; and fully expecting Alan would simply find another place to sit and read.

"Maybe I need the sunlight too," he mumbled under his breath, not really caring if she heard. Alan knew his wife loved her plants and flowers. In college she had majored in horticulture, and now that their two children were grown and married, the house plants became "her children." At times he resented all the attention she lavished on the plants. He pulled a dining room chair away from the table and moved it as close as possible to the window, turned and adjusted it so the sunlight was just right. He picked up his book and read the inside jacket cover. Oh, yeah, this was going to be a good one!

Alan had a home library with shelves full of books on history, theology, and biblical studies. His work as a pastor required both intellectual competence and relational skills. For relaxation, however, spy novels and international intrigue is what he enjoyed most.

Alan could hear Traci, busy in the kitchen preparing something for Saturday evening supper. They had been married for almost twenty-five years, for the most part, good years. Recently it seemed their relationship was strained, but Alan couldn't put his finger on exactly what was wrong. After reading a few pages he began sneezing. He blew his nose and noticed his eyes watering as well. More sneezing. "These plants are driving me crazy!" he yelled again.

"It's probably the orchid I got yesterday. It's really lovely with all its blossoms, but some people are allergic to them," she hollered back sweetly.

Alan put his book down and blew again. He was somewhat irritated with himself for yelling. Traci is so good about fixing meals, and decorating our home. And I do like the plants . . . most of the time. Or at least some of the plants . . . most of the time. He picked up the book and read to the end of chapter one. He was just starting the second chapter when Traci hollered from the kitchen, "Dinner's ready! Come and get it!" He closed the book and promised himself he'd be more appreciative of her during the meal.

The baked ham and roasted potatoes were fabulous. Alan thanked her profusely and sincerely. They were debating about having dessert now or later when the phone rang. Traci was already standing, so she grabbed the phone.

"Oh, hi, sweetheart!" "It's Tammy," she whispered to Alan. Their daughter had been married about three years, and so far, there had been no announcement about expecting a baby. Alan listened a few moments wondering why Tammy had called. "Well, we don't have anything definite planned yet," Traci replied, "but your dad and I are thinking maybe a trip overseas, since it's our twenty-fifth anniversary."

Alan felt a twinge of irritation again. Traci had mentioned a cruise or overseas trip about a month ago, but he had responded there was no way they could afford that. Now, without further discussion, she was talking to Tammy about her idea. Should he go in the den and grab the other phone? No, he hadn't been invited to join the conversation. He got up and started clearing the dishes to the sink. Whatever their daughter was saying, Traci sounded excited, but he wasn't sure what Tammy had proposed. After a few minutes his wife hung up the phone and said to Alan, "Guess what?"

"Something about our anniversary, I suppose," Alan replied.

"Yes! Tammy said she and Jim have been talking about our anniversary, and wondering what to buy for us, or if they can chip in on a cruise or any other travel plans we might make. Isn't it wonderful to have grown kids who love us so much they want to give us a generous gift?"

"Yeah, it's great! And I'm glad they both have jobs that pay pretty well. I know I wasn't making that much at their age."

"Well, where do you want to go?" Traci asked.

"I don't know. Almost anywhere would be fine with me. As long as we can afford it."

"Tammy had a great idea. She suggested that we go to Madagascar."

"Madagascar? Where in the world is *that*?"

"You know. It's a large island off the east coast of Africa."

"Why on earth would we want to go there?"

"Because it's an island, and has flora and fauna that is found nowhere else on earth!" Traci said excitedly. "Tammy knows how I love to learn about flora different from what we have here."

"Oh, right. You and your plants," Alan replied with obvious sarcasm.

"Alan!" Traci scowled.

"I'm sorry. I shouldn't have said that. I know you love to learn about new plants and flowers. I shouldn't be so selfish. Any change of scenery would probably be good for me," Alan admitted.

"Let's do a little on-line research and see what we can learn about Madagascar. I think that's where they have baobabs!"

"What the hell are baobabs? Poisonous snakes?" Alan looked horrified.

"No, silly. Those are the amazing trees that look kind of like palm trees, tall poles but with a normal looking tree on top. Some people say they look like an upside down tree."

"Maybe doing some vacation planning would help my mood. I'm sorry if I've been a little grouchy lately. I guess I could use some time away."

"We both could." Traci agreed. "Ooo, ooo! I just remembered. I'll have to ask someone to come in and water the flowers while we're gone. It's a shame Tammy lives so far away. I'd hate to ask her to drive several hours here and then several hours back home again."

"What about Barbara next door? We've looked after their dog when they're gone a day or two."

"Not a bad suggestion. And maybe Jerry would mow the lawn once or twice."

The following August, the plans were complete. Jerry had agreed to water and mow, and even take them to the airport. They checked their bags, and with passports in hand, boarded the plane bound for Dar es Salaam in Tanzania, then on to Madagascar.

CHAPTER 2

A WEEK IN MADAGASCAR

———✕———

"OH MY GOSH, IT'S BEAUTIFUL!"** Alan exclaimed as
soon as they stepped outside the airport in Antananarivo.
The colorful capital city was built on rolling hills. They
quickly spotted a van with the name of their hotel. The driver greeted
them in French, then, seeing the puzzled look on their faces, spoke in
English, and helped load their bags. Fifteen minutes later they were at
the hotel. The concierge was friendly and they were soon unpacking in
their spacious room with a view overlooking the small lake in the center
of the city. While Traci hung up some of their clothes, Alan flopped
onto the bed. "Jet-lag's got me," he sighed. "Why don't we grab a nap
before dinner?" In a matter of minutes both were sound asleep.

After a short nap and a shower, they went downstairs. The hotel
had a small restaurant off the lobby which served some fine French
cuisine. Prices were listed in ariary, the local currency, and in francs.
Alan wondered if the prices were high (the number of ariary looked

outrageous), but simply asked the waiter to charge it to their hotel room. Back in their room that evening, they poured over the brochures they had brought from home. Their travel agent had recommended at least two days in Antananarivo, to get acclimated and rested from the trip. The plan was to spend two days in the capital before exploring the island. They would travel first to Ranomafana National Park, then spend a day at Isalo, another popular national park. After hiking and driving for several days they would come back to Antananarivo, board a plane that would take them to the coast for two final days of relaxation before flying home at the end of the week.

Early the next morning, the sun shone brightly through the hotel window waking them briefly, but they agreed to see if they could sleep another hour. Nearly two hours later they rolled out of bed, dressed, and went downstairs for breakfast.

With help from the friendly concierge they discussed various restaurants, shops, and sights in the city. Traci pulled a highlighter from her purse and drew lines on a map for a walking tour of the city. Alan was anxious to get going, and Traci agreed they needed the exercise after spending so many hours on the plane.

Their first stop, a few blocks from the hotel, was a local bank. There they exchanged a couple hundred dollars in American currency for ariary. After strolling through the city for about forty-five minutes they found themselves in a peaceful city park. An open park bench provided an opportunity to sit and soak in the environment. Traci's attention went to the interesting trees and bushes; most were unfamiliar to her. Alan was watching a group of boys playing a casual game of soccer. There were no goals visible, but the kids seemed to be having fun just kicking the ball back and forth across the field.

"Isn't this great?" Traci pondered. "I think we're both so relaxed. Do you miss your office?" she asked sarcastically.

"Not much," Alan laughed. The pressure of his work was challenging at best and a real nightmare when crises appeared.

"I'm glad I got those two weddings done before we left. Those rehearsals and ceremonies were driving me crazy!"

"I thought *my house plants* were driving you crazy," Traci teased.

"Oh yeah, those too. By the way, do you think you can live a week without them?" Alan teased in turn.

"I think so. But Barbara better follow the instructions I left or I'll be furious."

Alan pointed to a nearby tree. "Is that one of those baobabs?"

"Good for you!" Traci nearly shouted. "You'll get the hang of this yet."

"Happy Anniversary, honey," he replied, smiling.

"Happy Anniversary to you too! Where should we go next?"

"How about some lunch?" Alan asked.

"Sounds good." Traci said as they rose from the bench.

They returned to the hotel that evening, tired, full from dinner, and feeling more content than they had felt in years. At the hotel desk they inquired about a tour guide for the next day. The concierge promised to have a guide to meet them at nine a.m.

The next morning, they were met in the lobby by the guide, Arwa, who had been called by the concierge. She spoke exceptionally fine English and bragged for several minutes about the many Americans she had shown around the city. She explained that Arwa meant "beautiful" in Malagasy.

Soon, it was off to the local market where shops of all kinds lined the street for blocks. They browsed for hours, Traci dragging her feet as they meandered past a bakery and a florist shop, while Alan was anxious to find souvenirs to bring home for Tammy and Jim, and something for Charlie their bachelor son. He also wanted to get a few small gifts for his friends at work. One of the flower shops had a display outside with the most unusual potted plants. Traci obviously wanted to linger, so Alan excused himself and said he'd be back in fifteen or twenty minutes. Traci and Arwa stepped through the door. They spent fifteen or twenty minutes wandering about the shop until Alan reappeared. He was excited to show them the stuffed lemurs he bought for the kids.

"Honey, our kids are twenty and twenty-three years old. Don't you think stuffed animals are a little juvenile for grown kids?" Traci asked with a frown.

"They won't mind," Alan answered. "Remember how they loved their stuffed animals when they were little? And what could be more Madagascar than lemurs?"

Traci decided not to make an issue of Alan's choice of gifts. "Arwa and I had a wonderful time browsing through the flowers. But I know they wouldn't let us take them on the plane, so I didn't buy any. I knew you'd be pleased about that." Traci grinned.

Early that evening Arwa dropped them off at the hotel. Alan checked at the desk to make sure the rental car for tomorrow's trip to the Ranomafana National Park would be ready. No TV tonight, they agreed. They snuggled into bed and before they knew it, the alarm was buzzing, telling them it was morning.

They dressed for hiking, tied up their boots, packed mosquito repellant, and headed downstairs for a quick breakfast. They picked up keys at the front desk, then walked out to the hotel parking lot where their rental car was waiting. As they drew near the park, Traci began reading from the brochure. "**Ranomafana,** which means 'hot water' in Malagasy, is doubtless one of the most spectacular National Parks of Madagascar." Alan turned off of RN7 onto RN25 and drove into the small village of Manandroy where they stopped for dinner.

They finally arrived at the Hotel Thermal Ranomafana that evening, and fell into bed exhausted. They spent the following day hiking through the forest, taking many photos, and finally returning to the hotel for dinner.

The next morning, they departed Ranomafana and drove to their second destination, Isalo National Park. Back on RN7, the road was narrow and often winding, so progress was slow. Alan didn't mind the slow pace, and Traci seemed relaxed as well.

Pulling the next brochure from her purse she began reading: "**Isalo National Park** offers some rewarding trekking opportunities, paths that wander past natural pools and through unique sandstone landscapes. The Sandstone Mountains have been shaped by the elements and date back to the Jurassic period. It is the home of amazing amphibians; a number of frogs can only be found in Isalo including the red frog." They stopped in Ranohira, ate lunch, and hired a guide. In a short time they were on the trail with their back packs, and heading up the steep slope. Alan was in his glory, taking photo after photo of the amazing rock formations. They returned to the car late that afternoon, and began driving back nearly 200 miles to Hotel Thermal Ranomafana. They arrived shortly after midnight and immediately crawled into bed. The next day they continued their journey back to the capital, Antananarivo, and checked into the same hotel where they had stayed before. Now, like the natives, they were calling the capital by its informal name *Tana*.

The final highlight of their anniversary excursion was a two-day relaxation vacation at a beach resort. The room was light and airy, the beach spacious and uncrowded. Alan and Traci spent most of the day lounging by the pool and sipping icy drinks. A second day was spent exploring the beach, and again, lounging at poolside. They agreed they had never been more relaxed in their entire life.

In the morning, they boarded a small plane, and returned to the capital. After deplaning at the airport, they hailed a taxi. Traci wanted to stop once more at the friendly florist shop in the market. At the florist shop Alan again excused himself to browse his way down the street, more for the exercise than anything else. Inside the shop Traci was welcomed again by the same shop manager who remembered her from the previous visit.

"Did you come back to order orchids?" he asked with his Malagasy accent.

"Not really," she replied. "I have quite a few orchids at home. I was hoping to find something exotic, unique to Madagascar, something none of my friends have ever seen before."

"Aaah, I think I may have something that will interest you. I told you before that many of our native plant species are used as herbal remedies for a variety of afflictions. The drugs vinblastine and vincristine are *vinca* alkaloids, used to treat various types of cancer. Now let me show you something really special." The vendor reached under the counter and held up a small paper envelope full of seeds. The picture on the envelope was of a bright purple flower. "This amazing plant will do well indoors. It only gets about 30 to 35 centimeters high."

"How high is that in inches?" Traci asked as she took the packet from his hand.

"Oh, about 12 or 13 inches. If you pick the mature leaves near the bottom of the stems, you can brew a tea with them, a tea with amazing healing properties. Even smelling the fragrant flowers will give you a sense of inner peace," the vendor claimed. "Each time you smell the flowers at home, it will take you back to your wonderful time here in Madagascar. Just don't let the authorities find the packet of seeds or they'll be confiscated before you even board the plane."

Traci paid the required ariary and tucked the envelope of seeds into her purse, planning to hide them in a corner of her suitcase back at the hotel. This was a gift to herself. She wouldn't tell Alan about it until they were home. "Happy Anniversary to me!" she sang as she left the store.

CHAPTER 3

GROWING PROBLEMS

"**WHAT THE HELL IS THIS?**" Alan asked as he pulled the seed envelope from the corner of the suitcase. The flight home had been relaxing, but tiring; and Alan could already feel himself tensing up before returning to work tomorrow. Traci was in the laundry putting the first load of dirty clothes into the washing machine.

"Oh, honey, do you have to start cussing the minute we get home?" Traci complained as she walked back to the bedroom.

"Where did this packet of seeds come from?" Alan asked, forcing himself to sound polite.

"Oh, those! I bought them as an anniversary gift to myself. You know how I love to raise plants."

"You bet I do," Alan shook his head, laughed good-naturedly, handed his wife the envelope, and wrapped his arms around her. "I'm

85

sorry I yelled. I don't want to spoil the wonderful mood we've been in. Wasn't that a fantastic trip?"

"It sure was," Traci agreed, returning his hug. "I enjoyed every day of it." She gathered up another pile of clothes and carried them back to the laundry room.

Alan was glad they had scheduled their return on a Sunday. He was confident the supply pastor had done a good job leading worship at church that morning. Now, he could return to the office on Monday morning, ready to begin a new week refreshed.

Traci got busy planting her seeds from Madagascar. She filled the divided plastic tray with potting soil and carefully placed one seed in each cup. There were no instructions on the envelope, so she pushed them down with her finger, covered each seed with 1/8" of soil, watered the entire tray, and placed it in the sun on the window ledge.

When Alan came home that evening, he didn't notice, or didn't comment on the tray. He read the newspaper, watched TV for an hour, and then turned it off. They talked about vacation highlights, went to the bedroom, made love, and went to sleep.

Each of them returned quickly to old habits, but both were in a better mood than before the trip. Traci was pleased that Barbara had taken good care of her plants, none had died. And within a month, she was surprised to see how quickly her new seeds had sprouted and grown. Some were already beginning to bud with strange reddish-brown flowers. Nearly half had withered and died. She had thrown away the envelope, but was sure the flower shown on it had been purple. Maybe the printer had enhanced the photograph, to make it look brighter.

As the plants continued to mature, she transplanted them into larger individual pots, fifteen in all. Traci was pleased with the fragrance of the flowers, but disturbed by their shape and color. Each blossom was like a bulb at the stem with overlapping, pointed petals that enclosed the stamen, leaving a large mouth-like opening. In fact, the blossom almost looked like an animal skull with fangs. She was certain that's not how it looked on the envelope. She wrapped the pots with paper and shiny brown ribbon, to compliment the color of the flowers, and began giving them to family and friends.

The first gift plant went to their neighbors, Jerry and Barbara, for looking after the house and plants while they were away. Along with the silly stuffed lemurs, they also gave a plant to Tammy and her husband Jim, and one to their son Charlie. Traci took five or six to church on Sunday and put them on a table in the narthex with a little sign that read: **If you like me, take me home.** They all were gone after the late service and coffee hour. Alan reluctantly took a couple of plants to the church office. He gave one to the office manager, and one to the janitor. Four remained on the window ledge at home.

One evening, shortly after dinner, the phone rang. Traci answered and told Alan it was Tammy. Alan muted the TV, continued reading the paper, and eavesdropped on the conversation. "He what?" Traci asked excitedly. "How terrible!" Suddenly Alan wished he could hear what Tammy was saying. Traci continued her comments, "Oh, that's awful. I can't believe it! That's not like him." Alan couldn't stand it any longer. Had Tammy's husband become violent? He raced to the den and picked up the other phone.

Tammy was just finishing the conversation, "So I've decided I'm definitely going to make an appointment with the vet tomorrow. Maybe he can tell us what happened."

"Oh, I hope he's going to be all right," Traci responded. "I know how you love that cat."

"Thanks, Mom. I'll let you know if I learn anything. Sure love you and Dad. And I'm glad you had such a wonderful anniversary trip. Good night, Mom."

Traci hung up and filled Alan in on the details. "When Tammy and Jim got home from work today everything in the house had been knocked over, torn apart, or shredded. Apparently, their cat went wild and began ripping into everything. Pictures and magazines were knocked off the end tables, even a lamp knocked to the floor. Every piece of living room furniture had been clawed. The drapes were torn. In the bedroom and kitchen, wooden cabinets had been scratched. Tammy said at first, she thought someone had broken in and trashed the place. Then she realized the cat had done all the damage. She said Buddy had been howling more lately, but has never been this violent."

"What do you suppose got into him?" Alan asked.

"I have no idea, and neither does Tammy. That's why she wants to get him checked by the vet."

"I sure hope they don't have to have him put down. I know how she loves that cat," Alan added.

Later that evening, Traci decided to try to calm her nerves after hearing about Tammy's cat. She pulled five or six leaves from the stems of her Madagascar plant (she didn't know what else to call it) and boiled some water for tea. The plants were now about two months old, and Traci remembered how the florist had told her about the calming, healing property of its tea. She crushed the leaves, placed them in a brewing strainer, and lowered them into the steaming cup of water. The fragrance wafting from the cup was spicy, and the taste of the tea was even better. It was spicy and perhaps a little bitter, so she added a spoon of sugar. She carried the cup into the living room where Alan was half asleep, his library book lying on his chest. Traci settled into her favorite chair and watched as Alan's head dropped even farther. She sipped the tea and found it calming indeed. Alan let out a little snort and his eyes popped open. "Why don't you go to bed?" she suggested.

"Why don't you go to hell?" Alan replied angrily. He resented being told what to do.

"What's the matter with you?" Traci asked. "You've been in a much better mood since our vacation trip, but the past few days you've gotten irritable again."

"Nothing's the matter. Maybe I will just go to bed." Alan dropped his book on the coffee table and without saying good-night, he went into the bedroom and went to sleep. Traci sipped her tea, wondering if something was wrong with Alan, or with her.

The next day or two went smoothly. Alan was pleased with how things were going at church. The fall Sunday School program was in full swing. He told Traci that several church members had thanked him for their plants. Traci was pleased to see her plants continuing to grow. Tammy had called to say the vet could find nothing wrong with Buddy, although Tammy felt she couldn't trust Buddy any more. And Jim simply wanted to get rid of the cat. Alan mowed the lawn on Saturday afternoon, and chatted briefly with Barbara next door. Traci made spaghetti for dinner and called Alan inside to eat.

Alan washed up in the bathroom and came into the kitchen. Traci stood at the stove, stirring the noodles one last time. Alan wrinkled his nose at the smell of spaghetti sauce. Usually he liked spaghetti, but tonight the smell made him sick. He picked up a ladle off the kitchen counter, stared at it, raised it threateningly above his head, and advanced toward Traci. "Alan, what are you doing?" Traci asked, frightened. Alan glared at her but said nothing. "Alan, stop it! You're scaring me."

Alan took another step toward her, shaking the ladle.

"Please, Alan, put that down!" Traci yelled.

Alan raised the ladle higher and suddenly swung it down hard against the sink. BANG! The kitchen rang with the sound. Traci let out a short scream. The plastic handle cracked in Alan's hand, and the ladle tumbled to the floor. He looked down at the broken handle in his hand and at the ladle rocking on the kitchen floor. He looked up at Traci with a puzzled frown. "What just happened?" he asked.

"I thought you were going to hit me with the ladle," Traci answered.

Alan looked again at the ladle on the floor and the plastic in his hand, now in two pieces. He set the plastic pieces on the counter and picked up the metal ladle and laid it in the sink. He noticed the dent in the stainless steel sink. "Oh m'gosh, did I do that?"

Traci was nearly in tears. "Yes, and I thought you were going to hit me."

It was slowly dawning on Alan what he had done. "I'm so sorry, Traci. I wouldn't hurt you. You know that."

"Well, that's what I've always believed. But that look in your eyes really scared me."

"I'm sorry, honey. I don't know what came over me. For a moment or two I guess I was just so full of rage, I didn't know what I was doing."

"Why on earth would you be overcome with rage?"

"I don't know. I truly don't know what happened. I'm truly sorry if I scared you."

Traci reluctantly embraced him, feeling that his apology was sincere. He seemed to be calmer now. And she hoped she would never see him like that again. She served the spaghetti, and they both enjoyed it. A cup of Madagascar tea also seemed to calm their nerves.

A couple of nights later, they agreed to finish the leftover spaghetti. Traci hoped once it was gone, the memories of Alan's irrational behavior would be forgotten. She warmed the sauce, boiled some fresh noodles, and they sat down to eat. Just as they finished eating, they heard an engine revving outside, and a squealing of tires. A woman screamed, and then they heard a loud crash.

They ran out the front door to see what had happened. Barbara was lying on the driveway next to the garage. Jerry's pickup truck had smashed into the garage even though the door was up. Steam was coming from the engine. Traci ran to check on Barbara. Alan walked quickly to the pickup as Jerry climbed out through the driver's door. "What happened?" Alan asked.

"I was about to ask the same thing," Jerry replied. He looked at the front end of the truck, then he saw Barbara with Traci bending over her. "Oh my God!" Jerry cried out. He stumbled toward his wife. Nearly crying, he sobbed, "I'm sorry. I'm so sorry. Are you okay?"

Traci helped Barbara to her feet. "Yes, I'm okay, I guess. What on earth were you thinking?" she said to Jerry in an accusing voice.

Jerry reached out to grab her, but Barbara pushed him away and moved behind Traci. "Get away from me," she sobbed. "You tried to kill me."

"No, no, Barb. I wouldn't do that."

"You ran the truck right at me!" Barbara screamed.

Jerry didn't know what to say. He looked at the truck smashed against the corner of the garage. He looked at Alan and then at Traci. His mind tried to process what he was seeing. "I don't know what happened," he pleaded. "I know I was mad about something. I remember sitting in the truck revving the engine and getting madder and madder." He looked again at Barbara. "Did I hit you with the truck?"

"No, thank God. You missed." Barbara was angry and scared. "I think you tried to, but I jumped out of the way just before you hit the garage."

Alan and Traci could hardly believe what they were hearing, and what they had just witnessed. They heard a siren, a police car or ambulance approaching. Apparently, one of the neighbors had called 9-1-1. "Barbara, are you okay?" Alan asked.

"I think so," she replied. "I just don't want to be around Jerry tonight. I don't want to be alone with him."

"That's understandable," Traci replied, "under the circumstances. Why don't you spend the night with us? Maybe we'll be able to make more sense of this in the morning."

"Thank you, thank you. I think that would be best. Are you sure it's not too much trouble?"

"No trouble at all," Traci answered as a squad car pulled up and two officers got out. "We'll stay with both of you until the police are through with their questions. But you will definitely spend the night at our house."

While the police questioned Barbara and Jerry separately, Alan and Traci stood nearby and had their own quiet discussion. "Do you suppose," Traci wondered, "that whatever triggered Jerry's anger is the same thing that triggered your outburst the other night? What do you two have in common?"

"With that jerk?" Alan responded, "Absolutely nothing!"

"I'm sorry, Alan; but Jerry is not a jerk. I've never seen him like this," Traci replied.

After a few minutes, Barbara refused to press charges against Jerry, so the police gave him a stern warning, wrote up the incident, and left the scene. Jerry apologized again to his wife, then went to do a closer inspection of the damage to his truck. Barbara turned away, still unable to believe what had happened. Traci walked with her quietly back to their house and ushered her inside.

CHAPTER 4

WHAT IS IT?

———⦿———

ALL OF THEM HAD TROUBLE FALLING ASLEEP **THAT NIGHT.** Barbara was settled in the guest room. Jerry was at home alone, still wondering what had come over him. Traci and Alan tossed and turned. The next morning, they watched as Jerry drove off to work in his car. A short time later, Alan also left for work. Barbara insisted she was okay, and after breakfast, went back to her house.

The sudden mood swings were troubling Traci. She couldn't help thinking there must be some connection between Jerry's incident of uncontrolled rage and Alan's. That afternoon, Tammy called. "Hi, Mom. I have some sad news to share with you."

"What is it?" Traci asked with concern.

"Remember the incident a week or so ago, when Buddy tore our house to shreds?"

"Yes, of course. Did it happen again?"

"I'm sorry to report, it did. Just a couple of nights ago. We woke up in the middle of the night to this terrible howling. Buddy was tearing around the living room knocking over plants; pillows were on the floor. Jim finally managed to catch him, but got scratched in the process. I held Buddy for a few minutes until he calmed down."

"Oh, Tammy, I'm so sorry."

"Jim says he's had enough. It was either him or the cat. So, yesterday I took Buddy to the vet and explained what had happened, and asked him to put Buddy to sleep. I picked him up this morning, and just finished burying him in the corner of the flower bed out back."

"I'm really sad. For you, and for Buddy. I wonder what made him act that way?"

"I have no idea, Mom. No idea."

After the conversation ended, Traci couldn't stop thinking about one thing Tammy had mentioned, "Buster had been knocking over plants." *Could it possibly be the darn Madagascar plant she had given to Tammy, and to Jerry and Barbara, that makes people lose control? Even Alan had been affected. No, that seems ridiculous. Still . . . how could this all be a coincidence?*

Before Alan came home from work, Traci sat at their home computer and spent nearly an hour researching *pheromones*.

The glands in our bodies naturally secrete fluids containing pheromones. Olfactory nerves stimulate the hypothalamus in the cortex of the brain which stimulates emotions. The pheromone scent triggers illicit emotions in the hypothalamus such as attraction, sexual desire, and arousal. Although plant pheromones have been much less studied than animal pheromones, they are involved in a wide variety of processes in the life cycle of many plants, particularly in sexual reproduction. Perfumes arose from plant oils with smells similar to animal pheromones. Plant oils with the strongest similarity to human sexual pheromones come from jasmine, ylang ylang and patchouli.

Traci said nothing to Alan that evening, but she was determined to learn more.

The next day Traci put one of her Madagascar plants into her car and headed for the State University. It took a while to finally get into a professor's office for a meeting. Professor Chung was a specialist in agricultural botany and plant pathology.

"Hello, my name is Traci Johnson," she said as they shook hands.

"Where did you get that interesting plant?" was his first question.

"In Madagascar," Traci replied as she placed the plant on his desk.

He leaned forward to study it closely. "Hmm . . . I don't think I've ever seen this species before. What is it?" he asked.

"I really don't know. I was hoping you could tell me."

"Well, it looks like a succulent, not a cactus exactly, perhaps a Cristate or Monstrose."

"The seeds came in an envelope with purple flowers," Traci responded. "But there was no name for the plant on the envelope. The flowers look creepy to me. And they're certainly not like the picture on the envelope."

"No-one really knows what makes succulents produce crested, fasciated or monstrose growths," the professor explained, "but they are fascinating. In many cases the aberrant growth may produce differentiated features such as hair or spines, or even flowers in this case."

"Are they dangerous?" Traci asked.

"No, not that I'm aware of," the professor answered. "What makes you ask that?"

Traci let out a deep sigh. She looked down at her hands which were fidgeting nervously. Perhaps it would be best to simply say a thank you and leave. "Well, I know this might sound crazy, but I'll try to explain why I came in. For the past couple of weeks there have been incidents of violence, or threats of violence, in homes where these plants are located. The persons affected are normally kind and gentle, but suddenly became very aggressive. I'm really worried. I'll admit, I'm scared by what I've seen." Traci took another deep breath. "I guess I was wondering if the plants might be emitting a pheromone that makes a person agitated or aggressive."

Professor Chung tipped his head and looked upward. Traci wondered if he was questioning her sanity, or just pondering the mystery. "Plants do emit pheromones," he replied calmly. "But usually they are intended for pollination, and have no effect on humans."

She listened and waited as he continued thinking and speaking. "Plants use chemicals to attract bees and other pollinators to their flowers. Some plant pheromones have similar chemistry to animal pheromones." He paused to think again before continuing, "I've heard that truffles, prized by some gourmets as aphrodisiacs, have an odor with chemicals that act as sexual stimulants in humans. I have one more question: Did all the situations involve aggression on the part of men, or males?"

"Yes, I guess they were all males," Traci answered hesitatingly, not wanting to say anything specific about her husband. "So, does that explain why my neighbor and my daughter's cat became aggressive and violent?"

"Pheromone stimulation still seems highly unlikely," the professor nodded pensively. "But you've really piqued my curiosity. Would you mind leaving this plant here for me to do a little research on it?"

"Not at all," Traci replied. "In fact, I was hoping, when I first came in, that you would say something like this."

Professor Chung smiled. "Well, I am intrigued by what you're suggesting. I'd like to investigate it further. How many cases are we talking about? Two or three?"

"Three so far. But if it happens again, or if there are any other situations, I'll let you know."

After a few further pleasantries, they exchanged handshakes and Traci drove home. As she reviewed the conversation, she wondered if she should tell Alan what she had done.

CHAPTER 5

A SPREADING CRISIS

———◇———

A LAN WAS IN A REALLY FOUL MOOD WHEN HE GOT HOME FROM WORK. When he sat down for dinner, his face was in a scowl. "I spent the whole afternoon at the hospital, waiting for old Mrs. Railer to come out of surgery. When she was finally brought to ICU, the nurse wouldn't let me in until they had her all hooked up to the machines. Then, when I finally got in, she was still so groggy, she didn't know I was there. So, I said a prayer and left."

"Did anyone say how the surgery went?" Traci asked.

"All the nurse would say is the operation took much longer than usual, so there must have been some problems. When I asked if she was going to be okay, all her nurse would tell me is that she was stable."

"The nurse was stable? Or Mrs. Railer?" Traci joked, hoping Alan would lighten up.

Alan gave her a sarcastic grin. "So, when I got back to the office, I started working on my sermon."

"Do you still have the Madagascar plant on your desk next to the computer?"

"Yeah! But I hate the ugly thing!" Alan gave his plate a shove and got up from the table. He sulked into the living room to read the newspaper.

Traci finished her dinner in silence. *It's got to be those plants,* is all she kept thinking. After she cleared the table, put leftovers in the fridge, and dishes in the dishwasher, she went to the living room, hoping Alan's mood had improved.

He looked up from the paper, "Traci, you won't believe what happened at the office!"

"No, what happened?" Traci replied as she sat on the sofa, fearing the worst.

"Well, I worked on my sermon for about an hour. I lost track of time and I was still feeling irritable about what happened at the hospital. Mary came in and told me she was leaving the office early because she had to take her daughter to an appointment." Alan paused.

"And …?" Traci waited.

"I picked up a paperweight off my desk and was about to throw it at her. I stopped, and put it back on the desk. She smiled and left. All I could think of was my outburst with the ladle here in the kitchen last week. And, of course, that incident between Jerry and Barbara." Alan paused to stare at Traci. It looked like he was about to cry.

"Alan, I've got to tell you what I did today," Traci said, somewhat reluctantly.

"Please don't tell me you went crazy too," Alan pleaded, half joking, half serious.

"No, but I've been doing some research on plant pheromones."

"Here we go with the plants again," Alan sighed.

"Well, I'm CONVINCED the plants are causing people to become irritable and aggressive," Traci stated emphatically.

"I want to say that's crazy; but I'm starting to wonder if you might be right," Alan confessed.

"Today, I took one of our plants to the Agriculture Department at the University. I talked to Professor Chung, and he agreed to do a study on the plant."

"You didn't!"

"Yes, I did. And now I'll have to call to tell him we have another incident to report."

"You're serious?"

"Yes, I'm serious. I won't give him any names; I'll just describe what almost happened."

"Do you have to?" Alan asked.

The rest of the evening passed quietly with no further discussion of the plants from Madagascar. Traci decided this new information was too critical to ignore, so the next day she called Professor Chung. "I wanted to let you know I have another incident to report," she spoke by phone.

"And I have some news to share with you," Professor Chung replied. "But you go ahead."

Traci told him about someone they knew who had a Madagascar plant in their office. The person had become quite irritable and nearly attacked and injured another employee. "I'm more convinced than ever that the plants are causing it," Traci continued.

"Very interesting," the professor replied. "Let me tell you about my first experiment. Yesterday afternoon, I placed the plant next to a cage with two male mice. They were in the corner of the lab with minimal air circulation. This morning when I came into the lab, one mouse was bloody and dead, and the other was alive, but bleeding from his right foreleg and paw. I'd say there was evidence of aggression, wouldn't you?"

"Oh my god!" Traci's hand began to tremble. "Now what are we going to do?"

"I'm taking the plant to the botany chemist for analysis. She'll collect samples of the atmosphere around the plant, and do a chemical analysis of the leaves and flowers, and odors or pheromones."

"How long will that take?" Traci asked.

"Maybe a week or two, I'm not sure. In the meantime, I'd advise getting rid of those plants."

"I agree. But that could take a while also. We know the people we gave them to, but they may have passed them on to others. Or they may not believe the plants are dangerous."

"I'll get the results of the lab tests to you as soon as I can," the professor promised.

"And I'll get busy trying to round up, or get rid of all those plants," Traci responded.

CHAPTER 6

GET RID OF 'EM

———— ∿ ————

"ALAN, WE'VE GOT TO GET RID OF 'EM!" Traci was nearly shouting into the phone. "I just got off the phone with Professor Chung. He did an experiment with mice, and the plant made one of the mice kill the other!"

"Honey, honey, calm down. I can't understand a word you're saying."

"One of the mice killed the other," Traci repeated.

"What mice?" Alan asked.

"Professor Chung's mice."

"I thought he was in horticulture or agriculture. Why would he have mice?"

"I don't know where he got the mice!" Traci hollered into the phone. "I told you he was doing an experiment. Maybe he borrowed the mice from someone else's lab. The important thing is, when he put the mice near the plant, it drove them crazy, and one mouse killed the other. Don't you understand?"

"Okay, okay, calm down. One lab rat killed another lab rat, no big deal."

"But it was the Madagascar plant that made it happen. I told you it was the pheromones!"

"Okay, okay, I get it. This experiment proves you were right. So, I guess you'll have to get rid of your new plants."

"Alan, don't you understand? It's not just MY plants! We gave them to a lot of other people."

"So . . . tell them they should get rid of theirs."

"Exactly. That's why I'm calling you. I need your help," Traci was exasperated.

"I'm sorry. I guess my mind has been on church members and their problems. I'm sorry if I was short with you." Alan realized again that in almost every conversation with his wife, he was irritable. "What can I do to help?"

"Alan, do you remember the night Jerry nearly ran over Barbara with his truck?"

There was a slight pause from Alan. "Yeah . . . I remember. It was pretty bad."

"And do you remember the incident when you nearly hit me with the soup ladle in the kitchen?"

Another long pause. "Did you have to bring THAT up?" Alan asked, somewhat peeved. "Yes . . . of course I remember . . . but I'd rather forget."

"Do you want anything like that to happen to any of our friends at church?" Traci asked.

"Of course not," Alan replied indignantly.

"Then I suggest you think carefully about how to tell our church members those plants we gave them are dangerous. We owe them an apology for giving them such a dangerous gift. And I hope nothing really tragic has happened. You can blame me if you want to. But the bottom line is, those plants have to be destroyed."

"Okay, honey, you're right. I'm with you now. I'll get the word out."

"Do you remember how many plants we took to the church that Sunday?"

"Aaw, geeez. I'm not sure. Five or six plants?"

"That's what I thought. But you also took two or three to the office," Traci replied.

"What about the ones we gave to the kids?" Alan asked.

"I'm calling them as soon as I get off the phone with you," Traci answered. "And I'll talk to Barbara. She'll be glad to know Jerry wasn't trying to kill her. Oh, I feel just awful. Why did I ever bring those seeds home from Madagascar?"

As soon as Alan got off the phone, he picked up the plant next to his computer, went out the door of the church and dumped it in the trash bin. He went back into the office to talk to Mary, and apologized for giving her a plant. "We'll have to write up an announcement for the church bulletin on Sunday, warning people that the plants are dangerous, and asking them to dispose of them immediately."

Mary said she understood, and suggested, "We should put the announcement in the monthly newsletter, and on our website too. In fact, I'll send it to everyone on our mailing list."

"Thank you," Alan replied. "Thank you for understanding. I am so sorry about all this."

That evening Alan was anxious to report to Traci, and to hear the report on her efforts with family and friends. "Mary and I got rid of all the plants in the office. We sent out a serious warning via email to all members, and we talked to several who assured us they'd get rid of their plants at home. We've accounted for six plants so far, and I hope we get them all."

"The first thing I did," Traci replied, "was take the three plants on our window ledge out to the green re-cycle bin. I dumped them into the grass clippings. They'll be dead before they're picked up," Traci declared triumphantly. "Then I called Tammy and had a long talk with her. I apologized for giving her the plant and explained how it was the cause of Buddy's outrageous behavior. When she realized what I was saying about the plant, she began to cry. And I cried with her. I felt so terrible that it was my fault they had to have Buddy put to sleep."

"I'm sorry, honey. I know you didn't mean for all of this to happen. You didn't know what kind of plants they were." Alan tried to reassure her, and tried to help Traci forgive herself. "What about Charlie?" Alan asked. "How did your conversation go with him?"

"Oh, you'll like this," Traci answered. "When I told him about the professor's mice, Charlie just started laughing. I asked him what was so funny. And he said he threw out the plant the day after he got it, 'cause he thought it was so ugly."

Alan started chuckling. "That's my son, all right. I guess he and his dad feel the same way about some of your plants!"

A smile crept across Traci's face. "Maybe you're right. I have gone a little overboard at times."

"What about Barb and Jerry?" Alan asked next.

"Oh, that's an interesting one. Remember the night of the incident, how Jerry said he didn't understand what happened to him? Well, Barbara confessed today that she didn't like the plant either. She had put it in Jerry's truck on the front seat while it sat in the driveway in the hot sun. Apparently, it released a lot of pheromones in the enclosed cab. At dinner, she asked Jerry to please take the plant over to his mother's house. Jerry's mom loves plants and has a house full of them. After dinner Jerry got into the truck and backed down the driveway. Suddenly he was filled with rage. He raced the engine, put it in drive, and sped forward into the garage door."

"It really affected him; man, I'm glad he didn't hit Barbara."

"Me too; but guess what happened to the plant?" Traci replied.

"Oh, yeah, I guess it was still in his truck."

"Right. Barbara told me that when the repair man from the garage came to tow Jerry's truck, he found the plant spilled on the floor of the truck, so he simply dumped it into the garbage can at his shop. Anyway, it's gone, thank goodness."

Alan stretched and yawned, "What a day! Man, am I tired!" Alan got out of his chair to head for the bathroom. "Wait a minute! Did you say you dumped the three plants from the window seat? I thought there were four!"

Traci thought for a moment. "You're right. I had four plants." A worried frown wrinkled her face. "Oh! Of course! I almost forgot! I took one to the university!" she exclaimed with relief.

"Has the professor killed anyone lately?" Alan joked. At least he hoped it was a joke.

"He said they would do a chemical analysis on the leaves and blooms. It sounded like the plant would be destroyed in the process. He knows it's dangerous."

"Okay," Alan sighed. "Let's go to bed." Alan smiled as he headed for the bathroom.

CHAPTER 7

THE FOLLOWING SUNDAY

T HE FOLLOWING SUNDAY Alan and Traci got dressed early and drove to church. A few blocks from the church, Traci reminded Alan, "Don't forgot the announcement about the plants we took to church last month!"

"How could I forget? It's the only thing on my mind lately."

The service went smoothly, and at the conclusion of worship, Alan read the warning printed in the bulletin -

WARNING! The free plants which many members took home from church a few weeks ago have been found to be extremely dangerous to human health. They are an invasive species and should be disposed of immediately. If you have any questions, call the church office, or Pastor Alan and Traci. Thank you for your cooperation.

Alan apologized to the congregation and emphasized that any and all plants be destroyed. Two people spoke to the pastor after worship to assure him they had seen the warning in the bulletin, and they promised to destroy the plant they had taken home. One woman approached Traci and told her she had seen the email warning and disposed of her plant.

In the days that followed, Alan and Traci waited nervously for repercussions. There were no further reports of unusual anger or violence from anyone at their church. They prayed that all the plants were gone. They prayed they would be forgiven for any harm they might have caused. Traci felt she had learned a valuable lesson about invasive species, and about purchasing gifts from unknown vendors in foreign countries. Alan did his best to forgive her and reassure her that everything would be okay.

One evening, as they turned off the TV, Alan said, "You know, I think I've been in a much better mood lately. I don't know if it's because work is going better, or because the darn plants are gone."

Traci laughed. "Maybe both," she answered. "You know, I've been thinking about my house plants. I love the aucuba in the living room."

"Which one's the aucuba?" Alan asked.

"You know, the gold dust bush. I love the shape and the leaves. And I can't believe it's nearly four feet tall."

"That one is nice; I have to admit," Alan replied.

"But I've also decided to get rid of some of the orchids and cacti," Traci continued.

"Why are you going to do that?"

"Just getting to be too much, too many. Ever since the Madagascar plants, I've decided we really don't need any more house plants. I've even decided to move the orchids on the window seat ledge to the kitchen. That way I can see them when I'm working, and you can have your window seat back for reading!"

Alan got up from his chair and gave Traci a long, warm hug. "I think maybe we'll be celebrating fifty years before you know it."

Traci kissed him and returned the hug with a really warm embrace. "Kind of reminds me of our honeymoon," she whispered in his ear.

"Or that night in Madagascar . . . on the beach," Alan whispered back.

With the celebration of Christmas that year, the Johnsons also celebrated an announcement from Tammy and Jim. Their first baby was due in June! And not to be outdone, bachelor son Charlie announced his engagement. "We're planning an August wedding," he emphasized, "because we know we won't be able to compete with a new baby!" Everyone laughed.

The following spring, residents on the edge of town were delighted to see the recently-covered city landfill blooming with dark purple-brown flowering plants, though their budding flowers did look strange.

NOT
IN
SILVERTON

An Old-Fashioned Murder Mystery

by Jim Bornzin

ADVENTURE FICTION - MYSTERY

NOT IN SILVERTON is an old-fashioned murder mystery. No one in the quiet little town of Silverton ever expected a headline like this in the local paper: LOCAL DOCTOR SHOT IN HIS OWN HOME. Pastor Alan Johnson listens to rumors from all over the city. When secretly threatened by the killer, Alan shares a clue with the police which helps them find and arrest the suspect. But is there enough evidence to convict when the case is finally brought to court?

SILVERTON MYSTERIES features fictional tales from the life of Pastor Alan Johnson and his wife Traci. Expecting to live a "normal life" in the small, quiet town of Silverton, Oregon, they are little prepared for the unexpected and unbelievable, and sometimes unwanted events that ensue.

CHAPTER 1

WHY? WHY? WHY?

I t's a small-town newspaper, but the Silverton Appeal Tribune still has a few avid readers. Some follow the high school sports; some like to read what the city council is doing. The paper is published once a week in Salem, Oregon's capitol, but covers the local news of Silverton and Mt. Angel. Bundles of papers are then brought to Silverton for distribution on Wednesdays. Founded in 1855 and nestled in the foothills of the Oregon Cascades, Silverton's pet parade and antique shops are about the only tourist attractions. In recent years, the Oregon Garden resort has also drawn visitors to the area. Residents like the slower pace and less traffic than the big city. Over a dozen murals decorate the building walls downtown. The Santa Claus mural states: "Silverton, the town that still believes." No one ever expected to see a headline like this one:

Local Doctor Shot in His Own Home

Dr. Stan Williamson, specialist at the OB/Gyn Clinic in Silverton, died in his home on Saturday, September 21, at the age of 55. The homicide is being investigated by Silverton Police and the Marion County Sheriff. Dr. Williamson was on the staff of Silverton Hospital. He had a successful practice in town for the past twenty-one years, delivering many tiny residents of the area. The grief-stricken family has no explanation for his death. The chief of police says it is too early in the investigation to provide any details. A memorial service will be held on Saturday, September 28, at 11 am at Faith Lutheran Church. Donations may be made to the American Cancer Society or the Faith Lutheran Scholarship Fund.

Pastor Alan Johnson received the phone call from Janet Williamson, calling from the hospital on Saturday morning. Alan couldn't believe what he was hearing. Stan's wife Janet was sobbing hysterically on the phone. "Can you come to the hospital, Pastor? Our son is on his way from Portland, but I'm a wreck. The paramedics did all they could, but when I got here to the ER they told me Stan was gone, and they couldn't bring him back." Janet sobbed. Alan listened, not knowing what to say. "I'll be there in a few minutes," he stammered. Janet continued sobbing. "I'll be there as soon as I can," Alan repeated, and hung up. He turned to his wife, Traci. "That was Janet Williamson. She said Stan died. I've got to get to the hospital."

"What happened?" Traci asked in amazement.

"She didn't go into detail. I just said I'd come to the hospital. Maybe he had a heart attack or something."

Traci gave him a hug and whispered, "I'll say a prayer for you."

Dr. Stan Williamson was one of Alan's closest friends and finest church members. He had served as Church Council president for several years. Stan was an OB/Gyn surgeon with a small clinic in Silverton. He was also on staff at Silverton Hospital where he delivered babies and performed other female procedures.

Alan parked near the Emergency Room, greeted the receptionist, and went quickly into the ER. One of the nurses recognized the pastor and pointed to the cubicle where Stan lay and Janet sat next to the bed crying. Janet looked up. "Oh, Pastor, thank you for coming." A nurse dragged an additional chair in for Alan.

"Oh, Janet, I'm so shocked. What happened?"

Janet took a few moments to consider what she might say. "I don't know. I really don't know what happened. I came home from the grocery store. I went to get some milk and a newspaper. I came in the door from the garage and put the milk in the refrigerator. Then I took the newspaper to the living room. Stan loves to read the comics. And there he was on the floor. I ran over to him and . . . . it was awful . . . his face was . . . I can't say it . . . It didn't even look like Stan. His face, or what was left of it, was all covered in blood. There was blood all around him."

"How awful. How awful. I'm so sorry you had to see him that way."

"They've cleaned him up pretty good here at the hospital. Let me pull the sheet back so you can see him." Janet stood up, gently pulled the sheet down from Stan's face, and started to cry.

Alan looked in horror at his friend. One eye was missing; one side of his cheek crushed. He put a hand on Janet's shoulder and said a short prayer. Finally, Janet pulled the sheet back over her husband's face. The next ten or fifteen minutes were a blur. A nurse appeared at the curtain and said, "He's in here." Stan and Janet's son, Jeff, slowly entered the room. Janet rose to greet him and gave him a hug.

"Mom, what happened?"

"Your father was shot, like I told you on the phone. I found him on the floor in the living room. The medics did all they could, but he'd lost too much blood. And they said his brain damage was irreversible."

"O God, why? Why would anyone want to kill Dad?"

"Honey, I don't know. I just know we have to say our good-byes."

WHY was the question that haunted Alan, and Jeff, and Janet, and everyone who knew the doctor. Why would anyone want to kill a good man who so humbly served the hospital, the women of the community, the church, his wife and family. Why?

Faith Lutheran Church was filled with mourners and extra chairs were put in the aisles for Dr. Stan Williamson's memorial service. His body had been cremated, and a private burial service took place that morning at Valley View Cemetery. At ten thirty members and friends began arriving at the church. In his sermon, Alan struggled with the question, why did God allow this to happen? "God did not want Stan to die, but loves us so much, God gives us freedom, even freedom to do evil. What motivated someone to shoot Dr. Williamson, only God knows at this point. It may be a question we will never have an answer for. In the meantime, we honor the life of a servant, whose healing touch and knowledge was a blessing to many. Well done, good and faithful servant!"

The next day, Alan led worship as usual at ten a.m. Sunday morning. He smiled as he welcomed everyone, but didn't really feel like smiling. Everyone was in a quiet and somber mood, based on the events of the week. Everyone expressed the same opinion. This shouldn't have happened. Not in Silverton. Not in this peaceful, happy little town. How could this have happened here?

CHAPTER 2

WHO? WHO? WHO?

The police department, with only a dozen officers, felt pretty overwhelmed. The chief of police had chosen his top woman officer, Sergeant Ann Hornbrook, to assist him in the investigation. Her gentleness was a real asset when interviewing the family and grieving members of the community. One of the county sheriffs was also assigned to the case. They had a 9mm slug from the crime scene. And they had found a few smudgy fingerprints on the inside of the front door handle. However there was no match with any previous criminal records. Interviews with the family were followed by interviews with clinic staff, then at the hospital. The only thing the chief could say was "the investigation is in progress."

Pastor Alan Johnson did his best to return to his normal activities. Most mornings he checked in at the church office, reviewed the work needing to be done, shared his schedule with the office staff, and made his rounds to the hospital. Each afternoon he tried to be faithful to his workout routine, stopping at Silverton Fitness before going home for dinner. Some days he put on his running shoes and walked or ran out Water Street to Water Mountains restaurant. The exercise helped release his pent-up emotions. But Alan couldn't shake the nagging question in his brain: Why would anyone want to kill Stan?

In conversations with his parishioners the same question often arose, which only made Alan more frustrated. One afternoon he called the police department and asked the chief if he had uncovered any motive for the killing? "No, not really," the chief responded. "Everyone we've talked to spoke very highly of the doctor." The chief was a little reluctant to share any information, and turned the question back to the pastor. "If you hear anything from your members or anyone in the community, please let me know."

All of Dr. Williamson's staff were grieving. They were uncertain of what would become of his practice, and uncertain of the future of their jobs. A large OB/Gyn clinic in Salem made an offer to purchase the Silverton clinic, and to staff it with one of their young specialists. Everyone on Dr. Williamson's staff was relieved but anxious.

Everywhere the pastor went, the same question was being asked: Why would anyone want to kill the doctor? And it was a question no one could answer. Alan himself was deeply troubled. Not only had he lost a good friend, but somewhere in this small town there was a killer. As a pastor he had always tried to be a "non-anxious presence." In numerous conversations with members of the church, and in meetings with various community groups, he simply listened. People need to express their grief. In his weekly pastors' group, he found colleagues willing to listen as he expressed his. He talked about Dr. Williamson's calm demeanor and the optimistic attitude he always brought to council meetings.

Alan hadn't talked with Janet Williamson for over a week. Checking in with her would give both of them the opportunity to express their continuing grief. He called and made an appointment to visit her that afternoon.

"Please come in," Janet greeted the pastor at the door. "Have a seat here. Or would you rather go in the kitchen?"

"This is fine," Alan answered as he moved toward the sofa.

"Please. If you don't mind, I think I'd rather talk in the kitchen. I had professionals come to clean the carpet here in the living room, but I still get sad just looking at the spot where Stan was lying."

"I understand," Alan replied. "I'll follow you." She led the way to the kitchen.

Janet poured two cups of coffee and placed one before the pastor. "I'm so confused, Pastor. Some days I think I know what I'm doing. And some days I just wander from room to room, or lie on the bed crying."

"That sounds pretty typical, Janet. There's no right or wrong way to grieve. It's just a really hard time."

"But how long am I going to be like this?"

"That's hard to say. Everyone grieves at a different pace. There will be good days and bad days, then good weeks and bad weeks. If it helps you to know, I'm having a really hard time myself. I always felt good just knowing Stan was involved at the church. He was a rock of faith and confidence. I knew I could always count on him."

"Thanks, Pastor. I know he thought the world of you too."

Alan listened for a while and then began his own line of questioning. "We all keep wondering why anyone would do this to Stan. With a little more time to think, have you come up with any possible reason? Did anyone have a grudge against him? Did he have a hard time with any of your neighbors? It almost seems like it was someone he knew, since he let him into the living room."

"Well, I don't think this means anything, but . . . last year, he and the neighbor to that side," Janet pointed through the kitchen window, "got into a squabble over the big oak tree near the property line. Mike kept complaining about what a mess it made in his yard and driveway. Stan loved the shade it provided for our house which kept it much cooler here in the summer. Last July, Mike got really hot and bothered. I heard him yelling at Stan about 'how sick and tired he was of cleaning up from the goddamn tree.' Stan finally relented and said he would have it taken down. He asked Mike if he would share the cost. Mike said, 'Hell no, it's on your property!' Anyway, after we talked it over, Stan had it taken down, and we paid for it."

"Do you think Mike could have killed Stan?"

"Gosh, I don't think so. But Mike hasn't spoken to us since." Janet sipped her coffee and thought about the neighbor.

"Come to think of it, Mike has talked about how much he enjoys hunting for deer. So I know he owns a gun."

"What about people Stan worked with?" Alan asked. "Anyone with grudges, or some old or long-time resentment?"

Janet thought for a minute. "Hmm. . . Now that you mention it, there was something that has bothered Stan for quite a few years. There's another surgeon in town who thinks he "owens" the hospital. Well, maybe not quite. That's a play on words. Stan said Dr. Owens was very possessive of the operating rooms, and always felt his surgeries took priority over everyone else's."

"Has there been any recent conflict?"

"Not that I'm aware of. I suppose the hospital staff would be more aware of that than I am."

"Did you tell the police about this situation?"

"No. No, I hadn't thought about it for a while. Stan hasn't mentioned it lately."

Both sipped again on the coffee.

"One more thought," Alan spoke again. "Is there anyone in your family, or in Stan's family, who didn't get along with him?"

"Heavens, no! He has a sister and brother-in-law. You met them at the memorial service. She adores her big brother. Years ago, we even took some vacation trips together."

"Hmm . . . well thanks, Janet, for letting me ask all these questions. Thanks for the coffee. I'd better be going."

"Thank you, Pastor. I really appreciate being able to talk about this. I keep thinking people are tired of hearing me talk about Stan. Before you go, would you say a prayer with me?"

118

"Certainly." Alan reached over and took Janet's hand and they prayed.

It was a bad dream. It couldn't be real. It didn't really happen. Not in Silverton. Not to a respected doctor. Alan had been a pastor for twenty years. He had performed nearly two hundred funerals, most for members of his church, and many for unchurched people from the community. None had the lasting emotional impact of this one. For the past week or two his thoughts had followed a different path. Surely in a town of only 10,500 people, someone knew who had committed the murder. Surely someone knew more than had been made public thus far.

With all of his contacts in the community, he heard nothing but bewilderment. It was a mystery. Sitting in his office one afternoon he acted on impulse and called the police department and asked to speak to the chief. He made an appointment for the next morning at the chief's office adjacent to City Hall. He was greeted cordially and asked to have a seat across the desk from Chief Mitchell.

"What can I do for you today, Pastor?" the chief asked.

"I think you're aware that Dr. Stan Williamson and I were very good friends?"

"Yes, yes I am. And that was very evident at the memorial service. You did a fine job honoring the doctor."

"Thank you. I'm here to ask if you would share any information you can about the investigation into his murder. I know there may be details you can't talk about, but can you give me a general idea on how the investigation is going?"

"Well, I'll be very frank with you, but mind you, this is confidential. I don't want this getting out in public. We've done a lot of interviews, talked to a lot of people, but so far . . . nothing. We're running out of steam, and not very hopeful about cracking this thing open. Mind you, we haven't given up. We'll keep working at it. Following up on any leads we may get."

"Don't worry, Chief, I will keep this in confidence. And I'm sorry to hear things have not gone well."

"Didn't we talk on the phone about a month ago?" The chief stared intently at Alan. "I think I asked you to let me know if you heard anything that might help us."

"Yes, we did talk briefly. And no, I have not heard anything. I guess that's why I wanted to talk with you again."

The two shook hands and Alan left the office and drove back to the church, as discouraged as ever. As he sat in his office at church he prayed, his mind going over his visits with Janet, with the family members, son Jeff, and Stan's sister . . . can't remember her name. Suddenly he remembered the elderly widow who had surgery this morning. He had prayed with her before surgery. He should get back to the hospital to see how she was doing.

Alan drove to the hospital, found the patient's room, and approached the door. Mrs. Murphy was in the bed sound asleep. He walked in quietly and whispered her name, "Evelyn?"

She opened her eyes. "Hi, Pastor."

"Hi, Evelyn. How are you feeling?"

"Pretty sleepy. The doctor said I did real well."

"Good. So glad to hear that. May I say a prayer for your recovery?"

"Yes, please."

Alan said a prayer and quietly left the room.

On the way out of the hospital, he stopped at the office of the Nursing Supervisor who was sitting at her desk looking at the computer monitor. The supervisor of nursing is the person who has the most contact with pastors in the community. Alan was pretty well acquainted with all three supervisors from his many years of hospital visitation. He was happy to see Shirley on duty today.

"Hey, Shirley, can I have a minute of your time?" Alan asked as he poked his head in.

"Sure, any time, Pastor. Have a seat."

Alan sat down, and after some small talk, decided to speak candidly. "I imagine you folks here at the hospital are missing Dr. Williamson as much as I am. Do you mind if I ask a few questions? Strictly off the record?"

"What's on your mind?"

"I'm frustrated, as so many of us are, by what might have motivated someone to shoot Dr. Williamson. You know the staff here pretty well. Is there anyone with whom the doctor did not get along? Are you aware of any strained relationship?"

"No, not really," Shirley replied. "I can't imagine why anyone would want to kill him."

"Okay. I'll be really direct, and please don't repeat anything I say. Let's just say I've heard that he and Dr. Owens had an occasional disagreement over surgery room issues."

"Oh, that." Shirley thought for a few moments about how much to say. "There may be some truth to that. Let's just say Dr. Owens has seniority, and he felt that Dr. Williamson occasionally ignored that seniority." After a brief pause. "But from what I observed, it was a petty issue that never escalated. At least not to my knowledge."

Alan nodded, weighing her words. "Is there anyone else on hospital staff who worked with them whom I could talk to?"

Shirley thought, then spoke, "You might learn more from Dr. Brauer, the anesthesiologist. He worked with both of them in the O.R."

"Thank you, thank you so much for your time. I really appreciate it." Alan rose to leave.

The next day Alan had his appointment to talk with Dr. Brauer. He was sitting in the waiting room of the hospital when Dr. Brauer, in hospital scrubs, approached him. "Hello, Pastor. Should we go to the staff dining area for our conversation? It might be a little more private there."

Alan sensed that Dr. Brauer was feeling some pressure, possibly from being called by the pastor and possibly because he was between scheduled surgeries. Or he could be nervous because he knows more than he told the police. "Dr. Brauer, I'm sorry to interrupt your busy schedule, but I have one question I would like to ask you about my friend, Dr. Williamson. I have heard that there was some tension between him and Dr. Owens over use of the operating rooms. Can you tell me anything about that?"

"I already told the police it was no big deal." Brauer's eyes shifted nervously back and forth. "Most of us doctors have egos. Dr. Owens was very sensitive about his seniority here at Silverton Hospital. Dr. Williamson was a very relaxed, laid-back guy. Very focused during surgery, but otherwise, lots of fun, always joking around. I think Dr. Owens expected Stan to clear everything with him, maybe to show him a little more respect. Just a little clash of personalities. I don't think it was anything more than that."

Alan nodded as he listened.

"We all loved Stan," Dr. Brauer continued, "But I certainly don't think Dr. Owens is capable of anything like what happened. You know what I mean?"

"Yea, I hear what you're saying." Alan nodded.

They spoke for a few more minutes, then Dr. Brauer excused himself. "Gotta get back to the O.R."

Alan sat thinking about the conversation. He couldn't get over the feeling that the doctor was covering up something, or knew more than he was willing to share. Now he had a decision to make. Should he make an appointment with Dr. Owens?

CHAPTER 3

THE PASTOR IS THREATENED

B ack at his office at the church Alan pulled several pieces of mail
from his box where the office manager had placed them. A
couple of ads for church supplies, a newsletter from the synod,
and a small white envelope addressed to: Minister. Slitting open the
envelope, he sat stunned as he read:

> *Mind your own damn business.*
> *If you don't stop poking around*
> *the same thing that happened*
> *to the doctor could happen to you.*

Clearly a threat on his life. He sat thinking for a minute. *Oh my
God, what have I gotten myself into? Should I take it home? Should I tell
Traci about it? Should I take it to the police? Right away or wait a day*

or two? He got up and started toward the door, then turned back, and with his hand trembling, pulled the envelope out of the waste basket.

"Sally, I've got a little errand I need to run. If anyone calls, I'll be back in about half an hour or so."

* * *

Cory was not in the mood to listen to his wife coo-ing and giggling over their infant daughter. Ever since she came home from the hospital it seemed all she could talk about was how excited she was about her precious baby. She gushed over how smooth the delivery had gone, and how nice everyone had been at the hospital. She still weighed a hundred and fifty, and there were ugly stretch marks across her belly. Cory thought after the baby was out, Beverly would return to her sexy self, and be ready to resume normal activities. But no. She was tired all the time.

What irritated him most was when she talked about Dr. Stan Williamson. How kind he had been, and how reassuring he was during her delivery. Cory remembered how pleased she was that Williamson was going to be her doctor. She had been working in the hospital cafeteria before her pregnancy. Even then she would mention how polite and kind and funny the doctor was whenever she waited on him. Williamson. The mention of his name made Cory's skin crawl.

"Honey, look how she grins when I tickle her toes!" Beverly tried to get her husband's attention.

Cory turned away from the window and his own private thoughts.

"Isn't that cute? I can't believe she's smiling already," Beverly commented.

"Looks more like a frown to me," Cory replied.

"Oh, honey. I'm sure she's trying to smile. Just think . . . this precious bundle was inside of me just a few weeks ago."

"Yea, yea," he answered unenthusiastically.

As Cory walked to the other room, he was struck by his wife's words, "this precious bundle was inside of me." *I wonder what else was inside of her. If she likes that doctor so much, why didn't she marry him?* Cory's thoughts were not making any sense, but reflected his insecurities and his jealousy. As he stood staring at his collection of rifles and handguns, his mind raced ahead. *Tomorrow is Saturday, probably the damn doctor's day off. He'll probably be relaxing in that mansion of his up in Abiqua Heights. Everyone up there has professional lawn service mowing their yard every week. Must be tough.* Cory picked up the 9 mm Glock 43 and carried it into the bedroom. He tucked it into a corner of the closet's upper shelf. *I'll think about it overnight and see how I feel tomorrow,* he thought, as he stripped off his clothes and got ready for bed.

The next morning Cory rolled out of bed. He heard the baby crying at 6 am but wasn't about to get up that early. Beverly had changed the diapers, nursed the infant for a few minutes, and tucked her back into the crib. Now, the sun was streaming between the blinds, so Cory dressed, tucked the loaded gun into his belt, pulled the jacket over it, and went for a walk. Beverly wouldn't wake up until the baby cried again, wanting to be fed.

He headed downtown to the local coffee shop. The small restaurant was full of patrons, usual for a Saturday morning. Cory ordered his espresso and sat on a stool in the corner where he could observe the customers. He also had his eye on the young barista.

Her flowing black hair really turned him on. *I wonder if Williamson got turned on, seeing Beverly in the cafeteria? And in his office, doing his exam of my wife's private areas.* Anger boiled up in Cory's neck. His teeth clenched tightly. *It wouldn't surprise me if the baby was his instead of mine.* Cory looked down to see his hand shaking and the coffee jiggling in the cup. With a hasty gulp he finished his coffee, took one more glance at the barista, and left the coffee shop.

Cory walked a block over to Oak Street then headed up the hill. It was a steep climb, but there was a cool wind blowing, and Cory's mind was already at his destination.

He turned off Oak and walked past the water filtration plant and into Abiqua Heights. Just looking at the homes made him sick and angry. He had the doctor's address in mind, and was certain the cartridge was in the gun. *Just have to see how I feel when I see the bastard.*

Ten minutes from the coffee shop, he climbed the steps of the doctor's house and rang the bell. A few moments later the door opened. "Yes, may I help you?" the doctor asked.

"Dr. Williamson, you don't know me, but you took care of my wife, Beverly Nichols."

"Oh, yes, how is she doing? How's the baby?"

"They're fine. But there is something I need to talk to you about."

"If there's a problem, you should take her to the ER. They'll call me if they can't answer your question."

"Well, it's kind of personal, and I really feel you're the only one who can help me."

"What's your question?" the doctor asked, becoming a little uncomfortable.

"May I come in?" Cory asked as he put his foot up and stepped toward the doctor.

The doctor backed up. "You really should make an appointment and I could see you at my office."

Cory shoved his way inside and pushed the door shut behind him. "Is your wife here?"

"No, not right now," the doctor stammered. "I do expect her back from the store any minute."

Cory reached beneath his jacket, grabbed his gun, and pointed it at the doctor.

"What's going on?" the doctor asked, both afraid and angry.

"You've been messin' with my wife, you son-of-a-bitch."

"Oh, no . . No! I'm a professional, and an ethical man."

Cory raised the gun, pointed it at the man's face, and pulled the trigger.

The Appeal Tribune came out on Wednesday. The death of Dr. Stan Williamson was the headline and front-page article. Cory was nervous. The following week, page three had a small article about the doctor's memorial service and the clinic's new management. Three weeks later, nothing. Silverton was ready to move on with events of the fall, school sports, and the new schedule for the city pool. Cory was breathing a little easier, and feeling there was no way they would ever find him.

Beverly Nichols went to the clinic for her six-week post-delivery check-up. There was a new sign next to the door with a different doctor's name. She was uncomfortable seeing a doctor she had never seen before. He was polite and professional, and after asking a few questions, said he was releasing her in good health. "Call if you need another appointment," is all he said. Beverly left the office thinking of Dr. Williamson and how much his calm, reassuring manner had meant to her during her pregnancy and delivery. She missed him terribly.

That evening Cory asked how her check-up went.

"Fine, fine," she replied. "I don't have to go back for any more appointments."

"Good," was all Cory had to say.

"I still can't believe he was shot in his own home."

"Yea." Her husband turned and walked away.

The guys at the auto shop where Cory worked were talking about the shooting. "Can you believe it? Right here in Silverton." "Do they know who did it?" "Man, you're not safe anywhere anymore." Cory didn't want to participate in the discussion, so he concentrated on replacing the carburetor.

"Hey, Cory, wasn't that the doctor that delivered your kid?"

"Yea, I guess so." Cory didn't want his buddies to think he knew the doctor.

"You guess so? Weren't you there in the hospital when the baby was born?"

"Yea, but things were so hectic, I didn't pay any attention to the doctor."

"Wasn't your wife seeing him when she got pregnant?"

Cory's hand slipped off the wrench and his knuckles slammed into the engine block. "Shit! Goddammit you guys! Can't you see I've got a job to do?"

His buddies returned to their respective stations and got back to work. But they were puzzled by Cory's behavior. They knew he was short-tempered. He usually joined in conversations about sports or hunting or what was happening in town. Today he seemed to be avoiding the biggest news to hit Silverton in years.

Cory was really upset. He didn't want anyone to suspect he knew the doctor. But that last question his buddy asked really triggered his anger. "Wasn't she *seeing him* when she got pregnant?" That was the suspicion that had triggered all his jealousy and anger. Of course, the other mechanic meant *seeing him* in the professional sense, but that's not what Cory heard. His anger seized him again. *I thought this would end it. Goddammit, why isn't this over? How long are they gonna keep talking about it?*

Beverly was at Visions, the local beauty shop, getting a permanent. She was finally getting a routine with the baby and found a neighbor willing to watch her for short periods of time during the day. Beverly realized she had been neglecting her own life. She noticed how messy her hair had become, and finally decided to treat herself to a permanent. The salon operator and a customer next to her were talking.

"Can you believe the police haven't arrested anybody yet for shooting Dr. Williamson?"

"I heard his wife is thinking about moving to Portland to be closer to their son."

"The members of our church really miss him. He was there almost every Sunday."

"Did you ever think such a thing could happen in Silverton?"

"You never know who's got a grudge or carrying a gun these days."

Beverly thought about her husband. He carried grudges and guns. She wished he didn't have so many guns in the house, but he insisted they were for hunting and for protection. The beautician came to check Beverly's hair. "I think the solution has been on long enough. Let's get you rinsed out." As she rinsed the chemicals from Beverly's hair she began talking about her pastor.

"Pastor Alan was really close to Dr. Williamson. He's been talking to everyone at church about it. He keeps asking how anyone could have disliked him. What possible motive could anyone have?"

An eerie thought about her husband prevented Beverly from saying anything. But she wondered if she should say anything to Cory when she got home.

Cory was in a pretty good mood that evening. He even noticed her new permanent and complimented her on how nice she looked. "Do the women at the beauty shop gossip as much as the men do at my barber's?"

"Oh yes," she answered. "In fact, today they were talking about Dr. Williamson's murder, and how awful it is that some crazy guy with a gun shot him right in his own home."

"Yea, that's pretty crazy," Cory pretended to agree.

"They said the Lutheran pastor has been asking everyone in his church if they had any idea who might have done it. He's even been talking to people at the hospital to see what they might know. I sure hope they find whoever did it. It's awful to think there's a killer loose right here in Silverton."

"Nah, it's probably somebody from Salem or Portland, looking to rob those rich people up in Abiqua Heights."

"I suppose. I hadn't thought of that," Beverly breathed a sigh of relief.

Cory went into the other room and looked at his Glock. *Yep, right there, locked up tight. Sure pisses me off that even the minister is trying to find me. I know how to fix that . . . right now.*

He walked into the kitchen and took a pad of paper out of a drawer. He sat down at the kitchen table and scribbled a note to the pastor.

> **Mind your own damn business.**
> **If you don't stop poking around**
> **the same thing that happened**
> **to the doctor could happen to you.**

He folded the note, pulled a small envelope from the drawer, and put a stamp on it. He pulled out the local phone book and addressed it to: **Minister**

> **Faith Lutheran Church**
> **1205 S. Center Street**
> **Silverton, OR 97381**

Cory thought about walking over to the Post Office, just three blocks from his house, but changed his mind. He didn't want his wife to question him about where he was going. So, he tucked the envelope in his pocket and decided to mail it the next day when he picked up the mail from their box.

The following afternoon, he stopped at the Post Office and was greeted by Mark, one of the regular postal workers. "Hey Cory, how's it goin'?"

"Pretty good, Mark. Say, what's the quickest way to get this delivered to someone here in town?"

"Well, if you put it in the slot there, it goes to Portland, gets postmarked and sent back here to Silverton for delivery. But if you give it to me, I'll stamp it. It'll stay right here and get delivered tomorrow."

"Good." Cory handed Mark the envelope who hand-stamped it and tossed it into a basket. "Thanks," Cory nodded. "I'm gonna get the mail from my box. See ya tomorrow."

Mark glanced at the envelope as he stamped it and was a little surprised to see it was addressed to the church. He knew the pastor pretty well, but he didn't know Cory went to church. He shrugged his shoulders and invited the next customer to come forward.

The very next day Pastor Johnson came into the post office. There was a one person ahead of him so he got in line. Finally, Mark called him to the counter. "What can I do for you today, Pastor?"

"Thanks, Mark. I just received this in the mail today, and it's postmarked *Silverton*. Does it look familiar to you?"

"Yea. I was here yesterday when Cory brought it in."

"You know who mailed it?" Alan asked in astonishment.

Mark leaned forward and spoke softly. "Well, I probably shouldn't have said anything. Privacy issues, you know. Sorry about that."

Alan responded very quietly, "No, no. I'm glad you slipped."

"Please don't say anything about this, especially to Cory," Mark begged.

"No, I won't. Do you happen to know Cory's last name?" Alan whispered quietly.

"Even if I did, I couldn't tell you," Mark replied. "But I thought you knew him since he was writing to you."

"Actually, I don't know Cory. And I think it's best I don't show you what was in the envelope."

"If he mailed something illegal, the Postal Service should know."

"Well, Mark, in this case, I think I'll take this to the police. I'll let them decide what to do with it. But I really appreciate your help."

"Any time, Pastor. Any time." Mark smiled cordially as Alan left the Post Office.

At the police station, Alan asked to speak to the chief, but he wasn't in. "Is there someone I can talk to about the shooting of Dr. Williamson?"

"Just a moment," the secretary replied. She rose from her desk and went to a back office. A few moments later, Sergeant Ann Hornbrook came to the front desk, greeted the pastor, and introduced herself. He introduced himself, told her he was Dr. Williamson's pastor from the Lutheran church, and then handed her the envelope with the note inside. She pulled the note out of the envelope, and couldn't believe what she was reading.

Her eyes opened wide. "Oh my God! This is SO incriminating! Do you know who sent it?"

"Well, to tell the truth, no. I don't know who sent it. But just a few minutes ago I was given a clue."

"A clue? A clue?" Ann was obviously excited. "Well, what's the clue?"

"It came from a man named Cory who lives here in town. But I don't know his last name. And I can't tell you where the clue came from, because I don't want to get that person in trouble." Alan smiled. This was all so crazy.

"I can't wait to tell the chief. He'll be ecstatic! Thank you, Pastor Johnson. This may be the break we needed. We'll follow up on this and be in touch. In the meantime, you be careful. And maybe do what the note says?" Ann grinned. "We don't need any more excitement around here, so you be careful. Understand?"

"Yes, I most certainly do understand. I promise to let it go, and let you folks take it from here."

"Thank you, again." Sergeant Hornbrook shook Alan's hand and he left the station.

CHAPTER 4

LET'S WRAP THIS UP

T he chief was ecstatic. The sergeant got to work. State Police records for gun registration were accessed to look for a match: 9mm guns registered in Oregon to an owner named CORY (no last name available). Ann Hornbrook began the search. She entered 9mm. . . Cory. . . and Silverton into the state records. She couldn't imagine how long this might have taken in years past, scrolling through thousands of registrations, looking for the first name Cory.

With the new records system, her search yielded results in seconds, several guns of various types and calibers registered to a Cory Nichols with a Silverton address. After a discussion with the County Sheriff and the city attorney, it was agreed they would speak to the Marion County judge about a search warrant for the Nichols' home.

Alan Johnson was extremely upset about the threatening note he had turned over to the police. He hoped they would be able to find the man who wrote it and take him into custody. At least they had a name now. He decided not to tell his wife Traci, knowing she would be a nervous wreck if she knew.

A few days after dropping off the note with Sergeant Hornbrook, Alan came out of his house to get the mail from his mailbox. He noticed a car parked in front of his neighbor's house, a car he had never seen there before. As he pulled open his mailbox, a movement caught the corner of his eye. He looked back at the strange car. He was almost certain he had seen someone behind the steering wheel rise up, look in his direction, and then duck down again. When he got back in the house, he made certain the doors were locked. He debated about calling the police; however, he knew Traci would overhear the conversation and go ballistic. He decided not to call. . . . just pray.

The search warrant was finally in hand. A team of officers went to the Nichols' home on Saturday, believing that would be the best time to find the suspect at home. They were right. Unfortunately, as the squad cars pulled up in front of the house, Beverly Nichols was sitting in the living room and saw the officers emerging from their cars. "Honey!" she called out, "There's a bunch of police coming to our door."

Cory was in the kitchen. He ran into the dining room and unlocked his gun cabinet, pulled out the Glock 43 he had used several weeks ago, and jammed a cartridge into the grip. He thought for a second where he might hide the gun but realized they would probably find it with a thorough search. Instead, he calmly walked into the living room, put the gun behind his wife's head, told her to be quiet, and waited. A knock on the front door was followed by a few moments of silence. Then, another knocking and an officer shouted, "Open up, it's the police!"

Cory took a few quick steps toward the door and unlocked it. He quickly stepped back behind his wife and put the gun to her head. "C'mon in, the door's unlocked!" he hollered. More silence.

Suddenly the knob turned and the door swung open violently. Officers came rushing in with guns drawn. They stopped suddenly when they saw the suspect with a gun pointed at his wife's head.

"Drop your weapon," the chief said, sternly but calmly.

"Or what? You'll shoot me?" Cory asked sarcastically.

"We simply want to ask you some questions," the chief replied, trying to de-escalate the tension.

"Go ahead, ask away," Cory replied.

The chief wasn't sure what to ask, but wanted to keep Cory talking. "I was going to ask if you own any guns . . . but I see you own at least one." The chief smiled hoping Cory would catch the hint of humor.

"Yea, I own several. And they're all legal," Cory replied.

"Cory, we really don't want anything ugly to happen here, so . . . please lower your weapon?"

Cory considered his options. He was badly outnumbered. He could kill Beverly, then take out an officer . . . maybe. Or he could possibly shoot an officer or two before being gunned down by all the others. Shit! No good options. The gun fell to the floor. Beverly started crying.

Officers stepped forward and snapped the cuffs on Cory's wrists behind his back. The chief "read him his rights," and he was walked out to a police car. The chief showed him the search warrant and went back into the house. He showed it also to Beverly. Sergeant Ann carefully slid the Glock into an evidence bag and sealed it.

The chief explained to Beverly that Cory would be taken to the county jail in Salem and after he was booked, she would be allowed to visit him. She asked why he was being arrested. The chief told her he was a suspect in the murder of Dr. Stan Williamson. Beverly gasped and began crying again. Officers confiscated the other weapons found in the dining room, recorded what they were taking, and began searching other rooms.

Ann Hornbrook suddenly had an idea. She knelt down in front of Beverly. "Mrs. Nichols, may I ask you for a sample of your husband's handwriting?"

"Why do you need that?" Beverly asked.

"Just an important part of a thorough investigation," Ann explained. Beverly rose and went to the kitchen. On the counter she found a short list of things Cory wanted her to buy at the store: shaving cream, Lava soap, and beer. She picked it up and handed it to Ann. "Thank you very much," Ann said. "And I'm sorry you had to witness all this."

"I guess it's your job," Beverly replied. "But I hope you're wrong. I hope Cory didn't do it." Her heart was breaking, but she had feared this very truth for many weeks.

The state crime lab proved conclusively that the Glock 43 owned by Cory Nichols had fired the bullet that killed Dr. Williamson. Cory's fingerprints matched those found on the door handle at the Williamson home. The threatening note, "Mind your own damn business . . ." was presented as evidence, written in Cory's distinctive printing. "The same thing that happened to the doctor could happen to you," clearly linked Cory to the doctor's death.

The envelope addressed to the "Minister" was not presented to the court. No one needed to know to whom the threat had been addressed. The evidence against Cory was overwhelming. His court-appointed attorney recommended he plead "guilty," which he did at trial. Beverly wept. Janet Williamson, and her son Jeff, sat with Alan and Traci Johnson. Traci held her hand when the verdict was read.

Pastor Alan Johnson was not called to testify, it wasn't necessary. He was thankful he helped bring a man to justice. He was sad for Cory's wife, Beverly. He was sad for Stan's widow, Janet. He was proud to have worked with Chief Mitchell and with Sergeant Ann Hornbrook. He was thankful for the small "slip-up" by his friend Mark at the Post Office. He was proud to be part of a "town that still believes." He prayed for them all. He decided to pray for the man convicted of murder. I guess **it can happen** in Silverton. He prayed for them all.

Silly
Serious
& Sermonic

Poetry by Jim Bornzin

LITERATURE – POETRY

SILLY, SERIOUS, & SERMONIC

The author makes no claims to being a poet; however, like most people, he enjoys some poetry, if it's not too sophisticated. The simple poems in this collection were written over many years, and reflect the author's love of humor (SILLY), philosophy (SERIOUS), and theology (SERMONIC).

The variety of styles and subjects reveal the author's diverse education in science and engineering, as well as theology and clinical pastoral education.

SILLY POEMS
Hawaiian Honeymoon
Limericks
Mrs. Jenner Ate Her Dinner
Arbor Harbor
The Christmas Elf
Free Verse
A Bow, a Bow, a Bow, and a Bow
"I" Before "E"

SERIOUS POEMS
Spring
There's a Bridge in My Hometown
Good Days, Bad Days
One Snowflake, One Man

SERMONIC POEMS
Sweet Grapes
The Story of Peter in Limerick Meter
Look at the Birds of the Air
Drowned in the Sea
Come, Taste the Wine
I See You in ICU
Creation Waits
Exalted on Earth

HAWAIIAN HONEYMOON
by Jim Bornzin

My new bride and I are a little neurotic
Our adventure begins with feelings quixotic
Off to Hawaii, a land most exotic
With luaus and leis and music erotic

The islands are lovely, pure and pristine
Peaceful and quiet and truly serene
The sky is so clear, the beaches so clean
Ocean from azure to aquamarine

The flowers are different, the fauna is too
The sauna is warm, the towels are blue
The pool is cool, the room has a view
The birds here cry, "Coo, coo, coo-coo"

A seaside resort, what a great place to stay
A room with lanai near the beach where we play
The garbage truck makes its rounds every day
Down the alley it comes to haul trash away

At six every morning, I give you my word
Awakened each day by this sound that we heard
Truly exotic, and somewhat absurd
The plaintive cry of "the back-up bird"
Beep … beep … beep … beep … beep

A tender young lass
from Poughkeepsie
Used to drink 'til
she felt rather tipsy
And if that weren't
enough
She even chewed snuff
Then ran off with
a traveling gypsy!

There was a young man
from LaGrange
Who did an abrupt
career change
Engineer he was not
Liked theology a lot
Though being a pastor
felt strange.

MRS. JENNER ATE HER DINNER
by Jim Bornzin

Mrs. Jenner ate her dinner in the dark
Because their generator wouldn't generate a spark.
Mr. Jenner would testify to the truth of which,
"The lights I'd test if I could only find the switch."
Mrs. Jenner was the miss, taken to the ball,
When both were young and quite mistaken
By the mystery of it all.

Love continues to mystify,
And I'd be sad, you see,
The prom we'd missed if I
Had been a Sadducee.
We said our vows, she was terrified, she knew
Her gown would tear if I'd stepped on it. Whew!
We danced beneath white canopies;
But tonight we just opened a can o' peas
And ate together in the dark.
At least our love still has a spark!

ARBOR HARBOR
by Jim Bornzin

If I'd a known what I now know
I'd a planted the trees in Idaho.
But I got tired of all the snow
So I left my home in Idaho.
I moved to where there's rain and sun
A small coastal town in Oregon.
There I planted a beautiful arbor
Around the little Oregon harbor.

If I'd a known, I'm sure that I'd a
Planted not the arborvitae.
It grew so fast and grew so tall
It soon became a great green wall.
People laughed at our new arbor
And called our town the arbor harbor.
Folks soon came from near and far
Over the mountains and across the bar.
To see the "Arbor Harbor Arborvitae."

THE CHRISTMAS ELF
by Jim Bornzin

A Christmas elf from Nantucket
Each toy in a box he would tuck it
The time's drawing near
Hitch up the reindeer
There just isn't time to truck it.

So being a hard-working elf
He grabbed the toys off the shelf
He loaded the sleigh
And got out of the way
So Santa could fly by himself.

While Santa was out spreading cheer
The elf worked as he had all year
When he found Santa's candy
He said, "Ain't this dandy
I'm sure glad Santa's not here!"

The sweet-tooth elf from Nantucket
Would chew on the candy and suck it
With Santa away
He ate candy all day
Then threw up into a bucket.

Santa returned; the elf's anger burned
Santa yelled, "Clean up the stall !
Feed the reindeer some hay
And polish the sleigh
Then go visit the kids at the mall."

The old elf was feeling quite rough
And told Santa, "I've had enough.
Who made you the boss?
All year long you've been cross,
I'm leaving you, outa here, tough!"

Santa was tired and unhappy
In fact he was feeling quite crappy
So he fired the elf
Fed the reindeer himself
And lay down for a long winter's nappy.

The elf said to himself, "Why buck it?"
And knew that with any luck it
Would end in good fortune
He'd retire to a porch in
His old hometown of Nantucket.

FREE VERSE
by Jim Bornzin

Have you ever
Felt insulted
By some idiot poet
Who breaks sentences
In half
Arranges words
Vertically
Omits punctuation
So your soul will
Be touched
More deeply
And calls it
Poetry
Me too
Or should I say
So have I

A BOW, A BOW, A BOW, AND A BOW
by Jim Bornzin

Congratulations! Take a bow!
The time to celebrate is now.
You did it, though I don't know how
All I can say is a great big WOW!

You cleaned the boat from stern to bow
Removed each leaf and branch and bough
Through each cabin you did plough
"Till all was done, now take a bow.

Pull back on the arrow, draw the bow
Hand grip steady, heart beat slow
Hold 'er steady, don't let go
The moment of release you'll surely know.

You won the blue ribbon tied in a bow
With each win let your confidence grow
Medals and honors will certainly flow
For an archer in command of her bow.

"I" BEFORE "E"

by Jim Bornzin

I was in a rush the other day
When my neighbor stopped me, got in my way
I said, "I'm in a hurry and I need to go"
He said, "I've got a question and I need to know
How to spell 'receive' and how to spell 'relieve'?"
After I had spelled them, he couldn't believe
"How will I remember? They both sound the same."
I told him, "All you need know is in this little game.
Remember I before E, except after C
Or when sounding like A as in neighbor or weigh
Then there's seize and seizure and also leisure
Weird, height, forfeit, either and neither
There may be more, I don't know
But I'm in a hurry and I've got to go!"

"Thank you," he said, "you've made it so clear
Like the rhyme about days in each month of the year.
Thirty days hath September,
April, June, and November,
All the rest have thirty-one,
Except February which has 28,
Except in a leap year when it has . . .

Unfortunately, I was out of range and couldn't hear
How many days February has in a leap year
And how often does a leap year come?
Once in a century or a millennium?
Now, where was I going? Why in a hurry?
I can't remember, but I'd better scurry.
Wherever it was, I'm gonna be late
Guess I've just got too much on my plate.

SPRING
by Jim Bornzin

Energy stored and energy released
Winter snows in the mountains melting
Water flowing to valleys below
Earth's axis tips, the sun returns
Ground thaws, wind blows, sap flows,
Leaves, flowers, and love all blossom, spring!

The leopard slips slowly and silently
Through the tall thick grass
His gaze fixed intently on the gazelle
He waits, muscles taut
The tip of his tail twitching
He gathers himself to spring!

Setting his pipe in the ashtray
Next to his tattered recliner
From his faded overalls the old man
Pulls out his grandfather's pocket watch
Squints to check the time
And gently winds the trusty spring!

Through the mud the soldier crawls
Moving carefully toward the enemy bunker
Pushing forward on knees and elbows
Hands wrapped securely around his rifle
Still not seen, taking aim, squeezes the trigger
Releasing the firing pin spring!

Oh, the mighty Mississippi
Mother of the cotton lands
Gathering her children flowing from Montana
Missouri and Ohio, Tennessee and Texarkana
Trace her to her source in Minnesota
And you'll find a tiny spring!

Boy meets girl, girl smiles, boy melts
How long have you been waiting?
It seems like an eternity
I dreamed of the day you'd come
Romantic passion unleashed
Energy stored, energy released, spring!

THERE'S A BRIDGE IN MY HOMETOWN
by Jim Bornzin

There's a bridge in my hometown
A footbridge over the creek
On one side is the city park
With tall trees, cool shade,
Swings and slides for the kids
And benches, where grownups
Can sit and visit just for fun.
On the other side is business
With City Hall, the Library,
The Police Station, the cleaners,
Real estate office and restaurant,
Lots of hot sun, and traffic.

We begin life as a child
We love the park, the shade,
The slides and swings.
All too soon we cross the bridge
And go to work on the business side.
We cope with the heat of the day,
The labor, the competition, the rules,
The permits from City Hall,
And the traffic.

Some day
In the not-too-distant future
I'll cross that bridge one last time
Leave work and business behind
Walk into the cool shade
Of those beautiful trees
Become a child of heaven
Play with other kids
Sit on the bench
And talk with grownups
Maybe Mom and Dad
Just for the fun of it.

GOOD DAYS, BAD DAYS
by Jim Bornzin

There are good days and there are bad days
I suppose that's true for just about everyone
For the bum on the street and for the President
The day I found Socks was a good day
Or, I should say, Socks found me
I named him Socks like the President's dog
And he became my best friend
Rain or shine, he never left my side
That was a good day when Socks found me!

It was raining the day I came down with pneumonia
That was a bad day, one of my worst
Chills and fever, I never shook so hard
The days that followed weren't so great either
Sleep and shiver, shiver and sleep
I don't remember much about the next two weeks
Except that Socks never left my side
I guess I recovered or I wouldn't be here now
Those were bad days when I had pneumonia!

The day I turned fifty was a good day
The shelter was warm, the bed was clean
The day was sunny, and I felt "mean"
I walked the streets, I hiked the stream
I slept that afternoon in the park
And woke up to hear a robin singing
Happy Birthday to me!
My friends brought donuts and blew up balloons
My fiftieth birthday was maybe my best!

One of my worst was the day Mom died
I came home from school and found her
Passed out on the floor, I called 9-1-1
The ambulance came and they took her away
All they kept saying was, we're sorry, so sorry
Grandma said I could live with them
But they were too old, so I hit the road
Never went back to school, why should I?
I was seventeen, but I missed my Mom!

Spring and summer are the best
Walking the rails up into the mountains
It can be so beautiful sitting by a lake
Watching birds soar or seeing a deer
Gazing at clouds turning pink at sunset
Sleeping beneath blooming rhododendrons
Waking to the sound of a waterfall
Heart rejoicing at the wonder of it all
Good days when the sun shines and my bed is dry!

Mom used to tell me, someday you could be President
And I believed her, for a while
Until I got old enough to realize
Presidents have bad days too
Crises to face and tough decisions to make
It's the same for me, not much different really
Except the President has to stay in the White House
And I can go anywhere I choose
There are good days and there are bad days!

I miss Socks, dear God, I miss my pal
It started out a good day, we had a great breakfast
Thanks to some kind folks that fed us
Then we headed across town
To visit some friends we heard were passing through

I saw the car coming so I ran
I don't know why Socks hesitated
I can still hear the thud when he was hit
That was a bad day, Socks died in the street!

When I turned sixty I thought, damn, I'm old
I ain't young anymore, my body aches
Every day, especially when I wake up
Only time I ain't hurtin' is when I'm sleepin'
It's been a long time since I've had a good day
Even a bottle of booze don't kill the pain
Just makes me sleep a little harder and longer
Almost wish I wouldn't wake up
Maybe that would be a good day!

Today was a good day, I got a great idea
Maybe 'cause the sun was shinin' and the birds singin'
Spent most of the day in the park, 'til evening
Had a good talk with one of my buddies
Bought a bottle and drank it all, walked out to the bridge,
Lay down on the tracks and prayed
The train is due a little after midnight
I don't think I'll hear it
I hope I wake up, not hurting, birds singing!

Shortly after midnight, the engineer saw something
A body kneeling or lying, applied the brakes
Eighty feet later the train came to a stop
A call was made, but it was too late
The "street person" was dead
Was it a good day or a bad day?
No doubt, a bad day for the engineer
But for the proud beggar
Maybe one of the best days of his life!

ONE SNOWFLAKE   ONE MAN

One snowflake   One man
Tumbles slowly   Came humbly
From the sky   Into this world
Carrying in its unique   Carrying in his unique
And intricate architecture   And loving person
All the infinite care   All the infinite care
Of God in heaven   Of God in heaven
To the earth below   To the earth below

A design   A man
So beautiful   So concerned
And fleeting that   And so kind
Only an inspired artist   Other people
Could create such   Could not believe
A delicate sculpture in ice   Jesus was real

One snowflake   One man
Falls upon the earth   Came with light
Still warm   And warmth in his soul
From the long hours   To thaw the frozen hearts
Of summer sun   Of those who in hatred and fear
That now gives   Crucified the One
But a few hours of light   Who came only
To a chilling world   To love them

In a moment   In a moment
It disappears, and   He was gone
One tiny droplet of water   But not lost
Slides down   For God lifted him
A blade of grass   Back into heaven
And is gone   To show the world
But not lost   It was not lost, but forgiven

One snowflake	One man
Adds its moisture	Gave his life
To millions of others	For millions of others
Giving life a new beginning	Giving life a new beginning
When the warm spring sun	When the Holy Spirit
Once again comes to thaw	Once again kindles faith
The frozen earth.	In the Savior, Jesus the Lord.

SWEET GRAPES
by Jim Bornzin

Grapes, purple and plump,
Sparkling with dew in the morning sun.
Grapes, Sun-drenched and sweet,
Vine-ripened and ready for harvest.
Whose grapes are these?
In whose vineyard have they grown?
Who sent the winter cold,
Giving rest to the vines,
Dormant during winter's chill?
Who sent the spring showers,
Warming and wetting
Roots spreading?
Who sent the summer sun,
Energizing,
New leaves unfolding?
Sparkling, sun-drenched and sweet,
Whose grapes are these?

The earth is the Lord's
And the fullness thereof,
The sea is His, for He made it,
And His hands formed the dry land.
The sun and moon, and stars are His;
The dew and the rain,
And the grapes are His also.

How easy it is to forget and deny
That God is God and all are His.
It seems He's gone away
To some other country
To some other venture
An absentee landlord
Leaving us alone

Leaving us in charge
Leaving us to think it's ours,
The world, the vineyard, the grapes.

I have a deed; the house is mine.
I've taken a wife; crack open the wine.
You've got a title for your new car.
The astronomer's name is on his new
star.
The paycheck's yours; you earned it.
God claims a tithe; you've spurned it.
This money's mine; I'll do as I please.
This property's mine, and so are the
trees.

This is my land, my pond, my well.
It's mine to keep, or mine to sell.
I tilled the soil and dressed the vine.
The vineyard and the grapes are MINE!

Each time you place a coin,
Or a dollar or a check
Into the church offering,
You remind your forgetful,
God-denying self,
That everything you have is God's.
Your paycheck is God's way
Of giving you your daily bread.
Your home is God's way
Of sheltering you from sun and storm.
Your pension or Social Security
Is God's way
Of blessing your Sabbath years.

155

Your children are given to you
As a sacred trust
To nurture and protect
To bless and send forth.
Your grandchildren are God's way
Of reassuring you
There is hope for the future.
Your heart and lungs are God's way
Of breathing his breath of life
Into your body of clay.
Your days are God's precious gift to you;
How you treasure and use them
Is your gift to God.

When harvest comes
God will send his angels
To receive what is His.
Dare we think we can keep anything?
Come today to the Lord's table.

Come drink the sweet wine of God's
grapes.
Come drink the sweet blood of
God's Son.
Rejoice that the world is His, not yours!
Be glad that you can release everything
Into God's loving hands.

There is a place for you at God's table.
There is a place for you in God's heart.
There is a place for you in God's
heaven.

Grapes, purple and plump,
Sparkling with dew in the morning sun.
Grapes, sun-drenched and sweet,
Vine-ripened and ready for harvest.
Whose grapes are these?
THEY ARE THE LORD'S!
PRAISE GOD! THEY ARE THE LORD'S!

THE STORY OF PETER IN LIMERICK METER
by Jim Bornzin

A young man named Simon Bar-Jona
Had a fishing boat of his own-a
A worthy old skow
He loved her, and how!
He called her his dearest Ramona!

Simon was from Galilee
Made a living off fish from the sea,
No fisherman meek
He cussed a blue streak
He was human, like you and like me.

Simon and Andrew his brother
Were fishing one day like any other.
Jesus said, "Follow me;
Drop your nets by the sea."
So they did, which startled their mother!

Said Simon, "Jesus, when I'm mad
I find that I cuss like my dad.
I know that my mother
Said, 'Forgive your brother,'
If I did, would God then be glad?"

So Jesus told Simon this story
About a king in his glory,
Called his servants to pay
The debt owed that day,
The punishment promised was gory!

One servant fell on his knees
Begging, "Have patience, please!"
Said the king, "You may live;
Your debt I forgive;
Return to your family at ease."

So skipping along on his way
This servant, so merry and gay,
An old friend he met
Who owed him a debt;
He said to his friend, "You must pay!"

His friend begged him, "Please forgive?"
But he said, "That's no way to live;
To the prison you go
For the debt that you owe;
You think I have mercy to give?"

The king heard this story so cruel
And summoned the merciless fool.
"To prison YOU go
For the debt that YOU owe!
Don't you know the Golden Rule?"

Said Simon, "That man was a nerd!"
Jesus replied, "Have you heard?
Forgive more than seven,
I say, seventy times seven,
Then you will live by God's Word."

Simon, no fisherman meek,
Used to cuss til his deck hands were
weak,
But he learned a new way
Called forgiveness that day
Which the rest of his life he would seek.

Simon thought he was giving up fishin'
To follow a Man with a mission,
His old boat now leaning
No longer had meaning
Catching men was his new commission.

To Caesarea Philippi they came
Said Jesus, "You all know my name,
But who am I truly?
The crowds grow unruly,
I'm not in this game for the fame!"

"My friends, I'll put you on the spot,
Who do men say I am and am not?"
"Some say you're a king,
We're not sure that's the thing."
Said Jesus, "You're right, I am not."

Spoke Simon, who never held back,
"I think I'm on the right track,
You're the Christ, Son of God,
And though that sounds odd,
You're the Lord; there's nothing you lack."

Jesus' head had a strange kind of tilt;
He thought he'd find nothing but silt,
But while taking stock
Found Peter, the Rock,
"On such faith will my church be built!"

"To my kingdom I give you the keys,
This doesn't mean do as you please;
But love and forgive,
As long as you live,
And in heaven you'll find your ease."

Though a catcher of fish he had been
You've heard the story again
How Simon Bar-Jona
Said good-by to Ramona,
Became Peter, the fisher of men.

LOOK AT THE BIRDS OF THE AIR
by Jim Bornzin

Jesus went up the mountain to pray
It was much like any other day
But the crowds gathered 'round
They sat down on the ground
And waited to hear what he'd say.

Their crops were not doing well
And they had very little to sell
He saw they were nervous,
So instead of a service
A sermon he decided to tell.

Just look at the birds of the air
They seem to find food everywhere
They don't sow or reap
They just eat and sleep
So think how your Father must care.

Are you not of more value than they?
Do you not have some food each day?
It's not absurd
You're worth more than a bird
God always provides a way.

Consider the lilies of the field
What beautiful flowers they yield
These lilies tell a story
More than Solomon's glory
Of the faithfulness God can wield.

If God clothes the grass in lilies blue
Which fade in only a month or two
Which sprout from the soil
And neither spin nor toil
Will he not much more clothe you?

Your heavenly Father has understood
Even Gentiles need clothing and food
God knows your need
He is generous indeed
So why strive for wealth? That is rude!

Our faith is not based on a whim
Your Father wants you to trust him
So seek the Lord first
And your heart will soon burst
Into singing the words of a hymn!

In twenty centuries, the world's changed a lot
However, my friends, our worries have not
We still lie awake
And sleeping pills take
Afraid our wealth will vanish or rot.

Dear friends, don't you think we're the same?
Dazzled by power, wealth and fame?
I feel quite sure
No one wants to be poor
But wealth's not the name of the game.

You all know Wealth can deceive us
And sometimes good fortune may leave us
For wealth and success
Can make such a mess
And its loss can certainly grieve us.

The god named Wealth is a lie
The best things in life you can't buy
Goodness and love
Both come from above
For the kingdom of God we sigh.

So strive to love God and do what is right,
Get out of darkness and move toward the light.
Remember to pray
Every night, every day,
And you will be blessed in God's sight.

Can worrying make you live longer?
Does money make you much stronger?
Stay focused on heaven
And strive to be leaven
To worry just couldn't be wrong-er!

Here, today, Jesus speaks to his friends
Encouraging us to make amends
God knows your need
He is generous indeed
And now into the world he sends.

Work hard at the tasks God gives you
Do your best at whatever you do
Share what you can
Be you woman or man
Have faith, trust God, God loves you.

DROWNED IN THE SEA (LUKE 8:26-39)
by Jim Bornzin

I don't know whether to laugh or grieve
What the demons asked Jesus is hard to believe
The demons begged Jesus to enter the swine
If given a choice that wouldn't be mine
This wasn't exactly the Great Commission
But Jesus decided to give them permission
So the demons left the man and entered the pigs
Yet they were not pleased with their new "digs"
They rushed to the cliff and dove into the sea
And there they drowned as dead as can be

Now if you recall in times long ago
A leader named Moses to Pharaoh did go
Then from Egypt God's people he led
Toward the sea from Pharaoh's armies they fled
Moses lifted his staff and the sea made way
For God's people to cross on that fateful day
The Israelites walked on miraculous dry ground
But Pharaoh's armies in the sea were drowned
Much like the pigs in the Jesus story
I mean the demons named Legion, to God give the glory.

One more piece to this puzzle I'll give
The name of the region where those demons did live
Gerasa was known in every Jewish home
As the base for the powerful legions of Rome
An army base is also called a "garrison"
And Jesus chose to go to the country of the Garasenes
Garasenes, garrison, Garasa, and Legion
What did all of this mean for the people of that region?

Was healing for the madman something for which they prayed?
But when they saw the man made well, the people were all afraid.
You'd think they'd be so thankful, they'd even shed a tear
Instead, says Luke, they were all seized with fear
The story of the demons drowning left people without breath
The power of this Jesus guy scared folks half to death

The man from whom the demons went
Felt Jesus was from heaven sent
He begged to be with Jesus; he didn't want to leave
In his right mind now, in Jesus he'd believe
But Jesus simply smiled and sent him home that's true
"Go back tell friends and family what God has done for you."
So the man went away and proclaimed throughout the city
How Jesus used his power and showed him so much pity
"The demons are gone and I feel great;
To be respected again, I can hardly wait."

Jesus and his friends got into the boat
And back to Galilee they did float
They never returned to that strange region
But they never forgot the demons called Legion
And what does all of this mean for you?
Do you believe this story is true?
No matter what troubles or torments your mind
Jesus is with you and he's incredibly kind
His power can banish whatever ails you
Though problems be Legion they cannot assail you
Let them go to the pigs, let them drown in the sea
Jesus gives them permission to leave you and me

Fear not his power for good is its intent
To free us from demons Jesus was sent
Casting out demons and evil and ill
Such is our heavenly Father's good will

So go and tell others, the movement's begun
Tell people the good things our Savior has done
I've decided to laugh and no longer grieve
What the demons asked Jesus is hard to believe
The demons begged Jesus to enter the swine
It might make you think they'd had too much wine
Yet into the herd of pigs they were sent
And over the cliff all of them went
Your troubles and mine will all drown in the sea
Of God's mercy and justice and tranquility. Amen

COME TASTE THE WINE
by Jim Bornzin

Come taste the wine, the board is spread,
Come taste the wine, the Master said.
The life we live is bitter sweet,
The table strewn, not always neat.
A smorgasbord had been prepared.
We will not know how each has fared
Until the end, and last not least,
We sit at heaven's wedding feast.

Some scoff at what the Lord will give;
They turn their backs and never live.
Some practice quite a different trick,
They gorge themselves until they're sick.
Some scrimp and save, some buy and hoard,
Forgetting the graciousness of the Lord.
Each guest competes to get the most,
Have they forgotten who's the Host?

Come taste the wine, the living Bread,
Come taste the wine, the Master said.
The wedding feast was in high gear,
The guests hoped it would last all year!
Young and old they'd dance and shout
In Cana, 'til the wine ran out.

We all think life will be a blast,
But then find out it doesn't last.
Life gets hard, the marriage sour,
What happened to that joyful hour
When we before the altar swore
Undying love forevermore?

Priorities are rearranged;
The baby wants her diaper changed.
The husband wants the car repaired;
The wife just wants her feelings shared.
A kiss, forgiveness, and a tear,
The joy of yet another year.
Come taste the wine, the board is spread;
Come taste the wine, the Master said.

When joy is gone, what shall we do?
Whatever Jesus tells us to.
The servants did and to their surprise
A change took place before their eyes.

The water in six jars of stone
Had changed to wine by power unknown.
The steward said it tasted fine.
He thought it was the perfect wine.
Neither steward nor groom had slightest clue
Of the miracle which the servants knew.

And so it will be for me and you,
If we're among the faithful few
Who do what Jesus tells us to.
Go fill the jars, and don't ask why,
Obey the Lord who reigns on high;
And he will all your joy restore,
Who lives and reigns forevermore.
Go fill the jars, the board is spread;
Go fill the jars, the Master said.

The later wine the steward drew out
Was good enough to make him shout!
"Go call the groom and bring him fast."
"You've saved the best wine for the last!

Most people serve the good wine first,
And after all have quenched their thirst,
Their heads are light, and they won't know
If cheaper wine in vessels flow."

But here at Cana's wedding feast
The bridegroom seems to know the least
About the water, now the wine,
And why it tastes so very fine.
God always saves the best for last,
We'll learn in faith as years go past.
When we've drunk the dregs of life,
And faced each unimagined strife,
And all our strength is from us wrung,
We'll dream of days when we were young.

Yet this is not the end of story,
The gate of death opens to heaven's glory.
We'll see again in peaceful repast,
God always saves the best for last!
The wine we drink in our earthly home
Is only a foretaste of the feast to come.
A magnificent banquet has been prepared,
We will not know how each has fared
Until the end, and last not least,
We sit at heaven's wedding feast.
Come taste the wine, the board is spread;
Come taste the wine, the Master said.

I SEE YOU IN I.C.U.
by Jim Bornzin

I didn't see you
I didn't really see you
All I remember was a bum
Lying near the door
Of the building where I worked
All I saw was scum
I remember the black trench coat
Faded gray, dirty, torn and ragged
Like your hair, black, or was it
gray?
Greasy, long, and matted
You never got in my way
You had a scruffy dog
That licked your sores
I imagine you ate from the
dumpster
You couldn't afford the stores
I was hardly aware you existed
Yet I didn't like the fact that
You were there
You made me uncomfortable
So I looked the other way
I didn't see your sores
I didn't see your pain
I didn't see you.
At least not then.

I was too busy
On my way to the top

Of the building, where my
company
Was rising, not-stop
Because of my invention
So slick and so fast, soon
All of our competition was passed.
My design, I am proud to say,
Let me stand out in a crowd,
any day.
We started small, but then
Our market share kept growing
Our stock just kept climbing
My success never slowing
People said I was rich, admired
by all
In the business world
I stood, seven feet tall.

I was married for a while
To a quite attractive wife
But eventually she became
A drag upon my life
Though I gave her everything
She became a spoiled witch
The divorce for me was painless
And I left her fairly rich
Free at last to pursue my dream
Of climbing to the top
Success seemed so rewarding
I knew I couldn't stop.

You were there when
Things started changing
I remember the day quite well
The day God started rearranging
And my life began to look like hell
A stockholders' meeting was
scheduled
For two that afternoon
I came back from lunch in denial
Yet had a sense of impending doom
I remember my lunch didn't set
well
That my stomach felt rather queasy
I remember your presence
There at my door
Made me feel uneasy
The stockholders were angry
The Board of Directors in a rage
The value of our stock was falling
I tried to act the sage
I said, "It's only short term
We'll recover from the loss
Our development team can
handle it
We'll show 'em who is boss!"

You see, the competition
Had announced the other day
They would make the product
cheaper
And better in every way.

They moved ahead and did it
Their market share increased

Our share and stock went tumbling
It fell without surcease.

I used to drink to celebrate
The victories I'd won
I'd raise my glass, encouraging
My guests to have some fun.
But I began to drink alone
And fearful I became
It seemed I could no longer win
The competition game.
At work I grew resentful
Irritable and rude
I yelled at staff and workers
I was not understood.
The company was slipping
Needed someone big to blame
And soon the Board of Directors
Had settled on my name.
My job was lost, my fortune gone
My lifelong dream a bust
With nothing left, I sold my home
My life had turned to dust.

It's amazing how fast it happens
How quickly things turn sour
For several months I struggled on
Now, seems like just an hour.
Once again, I turned to drink
This time to ease the pain
I found myself outside a bar
At midnight in the rain.
My trenchcoat soaking wet
Pants with mud were spattered

I crossed the street to my hotel room
Somehow, nothing mattered.
I saw bright lights come at me
I heard the tires squeal
Then silence, darkness
Aa distant siren
Nothing could I feel.

They told me I was in the E.R.
I came to for just a while
I remember nothing else that night
Except… a nurse's smile.
In and out of a coma
For a month, or was it two?
Lines & tubes & pumps and drains
I lay in I.C.U.

It was there I had a vision
So real and so clear
I saw you lying near the street
I saw you shed a tear.
For me you cried
You thought I'd died
You saw me hit that night
You watched the ambulance depart
Your heart was filled with fright.

Suddenly, the vision changed
I saw you once again
This time you were in heaven
Surrounded there by friends.
The palm trees swayed, children played
On a beach of snow-white sand

I heard guitars and saw the stars
And lovers hand in hand.
I knew your name was Lazarus
This time I saw your face
I called to you and tried to tell
The torment of this place.
In and out of consciousness
I fought with stress and strain
Day and night and week by week
I tossed and turned in pain.

Then, one day, I wakened
In a new and different bed
I was aware of sunlight
And the pillow 'neath my head.
Out of I.C.U. at last
Awake and eating food
No more trache and no more tubes
Could life really be this good?
I bought a morning paper
From a lady dressed in pink
I skimmed the front page headlines
And just began to think
Of how much time had passed
Of how the world had changed
And how my life had been spared
Everything rearranged!
I laughed at all the comic strips
And before I called it quits
I turned the page and there I found
The space for the "obits."

I saw the picture of a man
Somehow I thought I knew
His name was Charles Lazarus

Could that, my friend, be you?
I read the short description
Of your life so brief and sad
Veteran of a forgotten war
A husband and a dad.
I couldn't shake the image
Of the bum, still in my head
I knew that I had seen you
Knew now, that you were dead.

In I.C.U. I saw you
It was there I surely knew
That you had gone to heaven
And the meaning of I.C.U.
Intensive Care they gave me
To make my body well
Intensive Care God gave me
To save my soul from hell.
Jesus is the sign of God's
Intensive Care for me
And now, intensely caring
I open my eyes and see.
No ambulance came for Lazarus
Who died outside my door

No ambulance came for Jesus
Whose love for me was more
Than I could ever hope for
More than I deserve
And yet He died to save me
That I might see and serve.

I'm working again at a full-time job
And volunteer down at the Mission
I see the men and women there
I talk of Christ's commission
To go and make disciples
To baptize and to teach
I realize that there are some
Whom I will never reach.
But now at last… I see them
As the friends that they can be
I'm willing now to look at them
For God …at last… reached me.
I don't understand the whole good
book
But this much I know is true
Jesus is God's way of saying,
"I.C.U."

CREATION WAITS
by Jim Bornzin

Struggle, Christian, struggle,
Climb that mountain we call life.
Don't give up, don't lose hope,
Face the pain and strife.

And laugh in spite of everything
In the face of a world that cries,
Today will be gone tomorrow,
"Thank, God," creation sighs.

Tomorrow will be glorious
In God's plan for creation,
And we will see that glory
In a sudden new revelation.

The struggles of the past will
vanish,
The present trouble melt away;
All will someday be completed
In what the Bible calls "that day."

Who knows how many years
from now,
How many eons may have wended,
When God's plan is completed,
His great creation ended.

The world is waiting eagerly
To see what is in store.
Attempts to tell God's future
Are guesses, nothing more.

Why shouldn't we be eager
If in fear and doubt we live
To see perfected glory
Which God alone can give.

Humankind, despite its sin,
I'm sure will seem quite odd,
When it is re-created
As "adopted sons of God."

We study evolution,
Trace life from ape to man,
And wonder how it's all a part
Of God's almighty plan.

Perhaps our life seem futile,
Not as we would have it be,
Meaningless and worthless,
One small link in eternity.

But thus has God ordained it
From beginning until now,
And still he does sustain it
Giving hope to furrowed brow.

What is this hope of Christians
Which St. Paul writes about?
It is freedom from decay and sin,
From fear and pain and doubt.

The scriptures say creation
Is in bondage to decay.
The scientists say entropy
Can only go one way.

Freedom is a wondrous thing
We taste it here on earth.
But the freedom of God's children
Will be completely new rebirth.

Though we may try to change the earth
With all our new inventions,
Each person still lives on from birth
With only good intentions.

God alone will free the earth;
He is our freedom song.
He will give true liberty,
And sort the right from wrong.

The hope is in the promise,
The promise in the Book,
And yet the wars and deaths go on
Everywhere we look.

A father groans in business,
A mother groans in giving birth,
A diesel groans and climbs the hill,
Where is the joy and mirth?

Will humankind die of freezing cold
When the sun has lost its glow?
Or will we all die in a land
Where radioactive breezes blow?
It all becomes quite real at times,
Hits very close to home;
We may be just as near the End
As Paul or St. Jerome.

So we sit today and wonder
Does it all make sense?
Perhaps the answer should be No;
We all are still too dense.

Yet we will be adopted
Though God alone knows how.
Christ may come on the wings of clouds
Or on a lowly cow!

And in his mighty wisdom.
According to his will,
The plan so long ago begun,
Our Lord will thus fulfill.

And then we shall see clearly
Creation's groaning cease,
If we have waited patiently
For redemption and release.

EXALTED ON EARTH, HUMBLED IN HEAVEN!

Jesus said: "For all who exalt themselves will be humbled; and those who humble themselves will be exalted." Luke 14:11

The envelope was parchment
Its edges trimmed with gold
It was addressed to me, of course,
My name in letters bold.

A banquet invitation
Or request to give a speech;
I tore the envelope open,
Perhaps a chance to teach.

"The honor of your presence is humbly requested
Please come for dinner at eight."
I wasn't surprised by the invitation,
Everyone wants "Jimmy the Great!"

My career as a coach has taken me far,
Just look at this wealth that's surrounding,
The size of my house, my cars and my boat,
My success has been truly astounding!

They'll probably ask a few words from each guest,
I've got a great speech on motivation.
I'll fill out this card and return it at once;
They'll be pleased I've made reservation.

Great coaching's a talent, a gift and an art,
So few have skills such as I.
Surround yourself with a good coaching staff
And the best players money can buy.

You've got to make them believe they're the best,
I expect a lot from my players and get it.
I make'em work hard, once they've tasted success,
I know they will never regret it.

So last night was the banquet; I dressed in my best,
And arrived a little before eight.
I don't believe in that society hogwash
About being "fashionably late."

I got out of my limo and walked through the door,
The hall was splendid, amazing,
The guests, a thousand or more, were milling about,
And each at the others was gazing.

I kept looking for someone familiar,
A coach or player I knew;
But no one I saw in the hall was a star
No wonder my confidence grew.

No Michael Jordan, no Tiger Woods,
No Harrison Ford or Bonnie Raitt;
No Alex Rodriguez, no President Obama,
Just me . . . "Jimmy the Great!"

They've invited the fans, their friends I presume.
I smiled my way through the hall,
Shook hands with my host, not meaning to boast,
Had no idea how far I would fall.

I took my seat at the head table,
The notes in my pocket were ready.
Slowly, the other guests took their seats
And our host with a voice clear and steady...

Introduced me to the person on my right.
"This is Nelson Mandela, reconciler of races,
Whom I suppose you've never met.
Would you mind exchanging places?"

Embarrassed, but still smiling,
I moved one seat to the right.
And next to me now was a little old lady,
So frail and so very slight.

"Please say hello to Mother Teresa,"
Was the next thing my host said.
And so I traded seats again,
And slowly hung my head.

Looking to the right once more
I knew I'd met defeat…
"Buenas noches, I'm Cesar Chavez."
So I moved another seat.

My host came back and spoke again,
"I know this may seem strange,
But this is Florence Nightingale
And you'll have to rearrange."

Guest by guest I moved on down,
My host at each chair bending,
And asking me to move again
Through hours never ending.

I was near the bottom now, as low as I could go,
One guest beneath me, a ragged, bearded bum,
With rumpled clothes and matted hair,
I'm down here with the scum.

My knees and hands were trembling,
Once again our host drew near,
He smiled reassuringly
As he sensed my foolish fear.

"I'd like you to meet my Son, the rabbi.
He understands your shame.
This is Jesus . . . Jesus of Nazareth;
I've heard you use his name."

To my surprise the hall was filled with laughter
As I began to cry,
The guests were laughing with the host,
At first, I wondered why.

And then it all made sense to me
I was such a puffed-up fool!
I had to fall . . . to learn humility;
I was invited to heaven's school.

The host was God, the bum was Christ,
I laughed until I cried . . .
And suddenly, I realized . . .
Last night . . . I up and died!

The veil between the here and now
And what will someday be
At times is quite transparent
Allowing us to clearly see.

We compensate for insecurity
By seeking wealth or fame
We hope at least our closest friends
Will not forget our name.

So if you think you've still got time
To make a big impression,
Remember that the Lord is near
God's kingdom is in session.

God knows your heart, he knows your mind,
He loves to see your face.
No matter where you are, my friend,
You're there by God's sweet grace.

We're all in this together,
No one above another,
And when at last God calls us home,
We'll all be . . . sister . . . brother. Amen

If you enjoyed this book, please read another by this author.

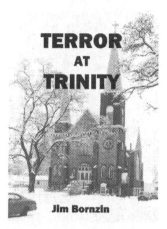

Terror at Trinity - Paul Walker entered a Lutheran seminary in the Midwest, young and idealistic, never suspecting his life as a parish pastor would introduce him to two kinds of terror: a holy terror from within, and unholy terror from an external threat. When the young janitor at Trinity Lutheran is found dead in the church, Pastor Paul Walker's life is thrown into turmoil as police search for the killer. Grieving church members threaten Paul's ministry and marriage. Years later, after sponsoring a refugee from Iran, the congregation is taken hostage by terrorists who threaten to blow up the church and everyone inside. Again, Paul wonders how he and the church can survive the terror at Trinity.

Tales from Trinity - Liz Sterling, church treasurer, is at work behind the scenes, seeking a way to discredit Paul and have him removed as pastor. Accused of embezzling church funds, Paul searches for help to prove his innocence. Mike Greenwood shares his personal journal. Mike's girlfriend dumps him in favor of the high-school quarterback, and then wonders how her life became such a mess. Meanwhile the pastor searches for Reiner Holtz, whose conspiracy theories have put him on the brink of insanity. In the midst of laughter and tears God's grace is pulling together a faith community of healing, hope, and joy.

BLESSED ARE THE HUNGRY

A Starving Artist
A Depressed Businesswoman
A Lonely Elderly Couple
Who Needs Who?

Jim Bornzin

Blessed Are the Hungry – A starving artist, a depressed business woman, and a lonely elderly couple live on the same floor of a Chicago apartment building. As they get to know each other's pain, struggles, and achievements, their lives unfold in ways none of them expected. The story reflects on the impact the people around us have in shaping and enriching our lives.

All are available from **iuniverse.com** or **amazon.com**

ABOUT THE AUTHOR

JIM BORNZIN is an ordained Lutheran pastor, married and living in Silverton, Oregon. In high school Jim considered a future as an artist like his uncle or engineering like his dad. These interests led to a bachelor's degree in Science Engineering from Northwestern University. See the poem *Spring*, exploring its various meanings. Working several summers in engineering convinced him he should  seek a career in something more people-oriented. What he enjoyed most at Northwestern were weekly theological discussions at the Lutheran Campus Ministry Center.

Jim decided to try a year of study at the Lutheran School of Theology at Chicago. After one year, he decided to go for one more. Then, a year of internship in a parish convinced him, this was his calling. His theological education includes a Master of Divinity, and later, a Master of Sacred Theology. He was ordained in 1967.

During forty years of ordained ministry, he served six congregations in Oregon, Washington, and Illinois. The writing of sermons honed his literary interests. Every year or two he wrote and preached a poetic sermon. Jim also served as a hospital chaplain in Spokane, Washington, and Silverton, Oregon; and as a volunteer police chaplain in Coos Bay, Oregon.

Retirement provided the opportunity to enjoy his many creative interests. In addition to writing, Jim enjoys painting, scissorcutting, and woodworking. He designed and helped build a hexagon shaped home, then wrote three novels, *Terror at Trinity, Tales from Trinity,* and *Blessed Are The Hungry,* all available from amazon.com or iUniverse. com. or his website www.jimbornzin.com. He went on to write several short stories and craft a number of poems, both **silly and serious**, which are found in this book.

Printed in the United States
by Baker & Taylor Publisher Services